D0272124

D 00 0004326

DOLLY EVANS

DOLLY EVANS

A *Tale of Three Casts*

Diane Keziah Robertson

Book Guild Publishing
Sussex, England

First published in Great Britain in 2011 by
The Book Guild Ltd
Pavilion View
19 New Road
Brighton, BN1 1UF

Typesetting in Baskerville by
Norman Tilley Graphics Ltd, Northampton

Printed in Great Britain by
CPI Antony Rowe

A catalogue record for this book is available from
The British Library

ISBN 978 1 84624 565 7

In memory of my parents
Jack Edward Hubbard
and
Elsie Lily Hubbard

Acknowledgements

To my sister Pamela, without whom I would be lost.

To my friend Eva, who during a glorious holiday in Cumbria asked me to write the first page, then the second, of a book I had had in my head for years. For encouraging me with Captain's Logs and for being an all round 'good egg'. And for not laughing when I lost the car. If it wasn't for her, none of this would have been possible.

To my friend Wilda. Thank you for loving Dolly as much as I do. My Encourager par excellence.

To Bill Donaldson. Many thanks for your advice and support.

To the team at The Book Guild. Thank you for your patience in working with this humble 'rookie' on her poor book.

To everyone who encouraged me, Thank You.

But most importantly, to my husband Campbell, the love of my life and the chairman of my fan club. Thank you for not allowing me to give up.

Diane Keziah Robertson

1

Dolly Evans, not having been shopping for two days, looked in the refrigerator and decided she couldn't put it off any longer. Taking paper and pen, she sat at the kitchen table and wrote a list with the heading 'April 28th'. She knew this to be so, having found the date on the newspaper delivered to her front door by prior arrangement with the newsagents in the village. She never actually read the paper, the day and date were all that were required from it, and besides it was extremely useful for lighting the open fire in the sitting room. For her last birthday her nephew, Robert, had given her a very fine watch, with a gold surround and black leather strap – it told not only the time, but also the day and date. There was even an illustration of the moon showing the phases, but she didn't need that; after all, she had the paper. When Robert came to visit, which thankfully was seldom, she made a note to remind herself she should wear it, not wanting to appear ungrateful.

Dolly needed to decide what to wear, but for that one had to know the weather, so she opened the door and stepped outside. The sun was warm for late April with not a cloud in the sky and, deciding that her new blue cardigan over a blouse and skirt would be appropriate, she went upstairs to wash and change from her nightclothes. Looking everywhere for the cardigan but not finding it she settled on an Aran sweater, a decision she would later regret. By the time she had collected everything she would need for this expedition – a shopping bag, her purse – the morning was moving towards eleven o'clock, but as she didn't wear a watch she had no way of knowing that. She closed the front door after her, but halfway down the front path she wondered why her feet were hurting. Looking down, she realised she still had her slippers on. Having returned and remedied that, she set out once more.

Dolly lived in Bowstones, a two-storey eighteenth-century cottage, on Sheep Lane in the village of Upper Markham. If she had ever thought about it, she would have realised that, in the county of Shropshire, Sheep Lane was a most appropriate name, however she had never given it a passing thought. She was born sixty-five years earlier in the second-floor front bedroom of the cottage situated on the estate for which her father was the gamekeeper, her mother working up at The Hall. Dolly's mother, pale and thin, had never had the luxury of staying at home with her newborn daughter, who was named after her maternal grandmother, and had returned to work a mere two weeks after Dolly's birth, taking the baby in a Moses basket every day, the small family not being in a position to forgo her pay.

Dolly's memories of growing up on the estate were numerous. Her parents had both been well regarded, and upon their respective deaths – her father from pneumonia caught while staying out in the rain trying to catch the all too frequent poachers, her mother five years later from septicaemia – the owners had told Dolly that she could continue to live in Bowstones for as long as she liked. A nominal rent was discussed and agreed upon, and the sum of twenty pounds a month was to be paid, which was fortunate as she existed on only her state pension. Even allowing for such a peppercorn rent, she still found it took a great deal of juggling to keep her greying and elderly head above water.

The actual village of Upper Markham was approximately a quarter of a mile from Dolly's cottage, but she found as the years passed it was taking longer and longer to reach it. Unless it was being moved further away annually, the only explanation was that Dolly herself was becoming slower. As she thankfully drew nearer the shops, she took out her list. The first stop would be the fishmonger, and she would make a decision on supper once she saw the selection. With the coast just five miles away the choice was usually excellent and she was very partial to fish. Her father, the gamekeeper, had kept the family well supplied with the usual rabbits, pheasant and quail in season, but she really liked fish best. The rest of her shopping would thus depend on what the village had on offer.

'Good morning Miss Evans,' said Tom. 'What can I get for you today? We have some plaice just come in, nice and fresh, or there's a nice piece of eel that would make a lovely pie.' Dolly settled on the plaice, and Tom Braithwaite removed the head for her without being asked, knowing she was a bit squeamish regarding that kind of thing.

'Thank you Tom, that's grand. How much?'

'Two pounds to you Miss Evans.'

Dolly handed over five and waited for the three pounds change, carefully placing it in her purse. Putting the fish, wrapped first in white paper then placed in a plastic bag to prevent leakage, in her bag she turned to leave the store. Unfortunately she hadn't heard Mr Milligan come in with his dog, and she tripped over the outstretched lead, landing first on her knees and then on her right wrist. 'Bloody hell!' were the first words out of her mouth as Tom came from behind the counter and

Mr Milligan hauled the dog closer. 'Are you all right?' asked Tom.

'No, I'm not,' she replied, and promptly fainted.

By the time the ambulance arrived Dolly was sitting up, her back against the counter, a glass of water in her uninjured hand and a blanket covering her legs. Tom and Mr Milligan were arguing over how many times Tom had told him not to bring 'that damn dog into the store', and Dolly was being administered to by Tom's wife who had come from the flat upstairs when she heard all the commotion. Quite a little crowd had gathered outside, unable to enter as Tom had locked the door and turned the sign from 'Open' to 'Closed'. With the noisy arrival of the ambulance, the rumour that had been circulating that someone had been shot appeared to be true to the outsiders, and when the door eventually opened and Dolly was removed in a chair carried by two hefty medics, they all thought it was she who had been thus injured. They were only partly right, and upon being told that Dolly had broken her wrist in a fall, with the fishmonger and Mr Milligan still shouting at each other, the crowd lost interest and dispersed.

At the Emergency Department of the local hospital Dolly joined the thirty-odd people waiting to be diagnosed and treated, her broken wrist not being considered as urgent as those with heart attacks, though Dolly would beg to differ had somebody enquired. It was therefore some three hours later that she actually saw a doctor. 'Does it hurt?' he asked.

'What do you think? It hasn't helped I have been sitting here for nigh-on three hours while you lot drink endless cups of tea. And why does it have to be so hot in here, I've been sweating blood waiting for you.' This ensured that she was kept waiting even longer, her file now identifying her as that annoying Awkward Patient.

Eventually, X-rayed and with bone set in plaster, she was told she could go home. 'How would you suggest I do that?' she asked. 'I live in Upper Markham.'

'Don't you have someone who can pick you up?' she was asked.

'No. Someone can give me a ride.' She was told she would have to wait another three hours for an ambulance to be available. Dolly's sense of smell not being overly sensitive, she had forgotten about the fish in her shopping bag, but the nurses, walking round sniffing various pails and containers of unmentionable things, eventually sniffed their way to her and asked what she had in her bag. 'Fish of course,' was the reply. The ambulance was available a scant fifteen minutes later and Dolly, at last, was on her way home.

One of the attendants helped her down from the ambulance and walked her to the front door. 'Where's your key?' he asked.

'I can manage,' she said, and so he placed her shopping bag at her feet, said 'Cheerio,' and he and the driver disappeared at a high rate of speed down the lane. As it was her right wrist in the plaster cast, she immediately found out it was extremely difficult to open the front door with the key, her language becoming more colourful with every try. Eventually it swung open, and she kicked the bag in before her. Stepping over it, she closed and bolted the door, walked into the sitting room and sank into the chair beside the fire.

The hospital had given her a small bottle containing eight painkillers, labelled 'Take one every six hours with food', also warning that this particular brand of pain medication worked quickly. 'What do they think I'm going to do with these?' she thought. 'Kill myself?' Making her way wearily to the kitchen, she filled a glass with water. If one tablet would work quickly then two would doubtless be better, so fitting the action to the thought, she went back to the shopping bag on the floor, took the fish out, which even to her was beginning to smell, and put it in the fridge. Deciding it had been one hell of a day she left everything, walked up the stairs and fell into bed, to sleep dreamlessly.

In the land between sleep and wakefulness there is a space where everything is right with the world, and Dolly lay happily in that space, letting the light slowly filter through her eyelids. Looking at the clock beside the bed she saw it was seven-thirty, but was unable to ascertain if that was seven-thirty at night or seven-thirty in the morning. Deciding that if she went downstairs and the morning paper was at the door, the problem would be solved, she found her nose beginning to itch. With her eyes closed she put her arm up to rub the offending body part. Unfortunately she had forgotten about her broken wrist, the tablets having worked well, and instead gave her nose a tremendous bang, bringing tears to her eyes. Looking at the cast, it took her a moment to recall what had happened to make such a monstrosity necessary. With recall came pain however, followed swiftly by the recollection that she had tablets downstairs that could help with that.

Hauling herself off the bed she saw that she was already dressed, which she considered fortunate as she had no idea how to cope with dressing herself with such an impediment. She made her way slowly and carefully downstairs. The remaining six tablets, 'Take one every six hours with food', looked very attractive in their bottle, and taking another glass of water she swallowed another two. Remembering that the reason for coming down-stairs, besides the alleviation of pain, was to check whether it was morning or evening, she headed for the door. The paper lay resplendent upon the doorstep, which meant it was morning. With no intention of picking it up or reading it, and caring less for the day or date, she went back to bed, taking two more tablets with her.

The banging woke her, and wondering who on earth was making such a racket, she turned over and pulled the covers over her head. The noise continued; her name was called. Finding her way to the window she unhooked the latch and looked out. 'What the hell do you want?' she yelled.

'Miss Evans! You're all right!' came the reply.

'Of course I'm all right. Why are you making such a row? You woke me up.'

'Miss Evans, it's Fred Stringer, Constable Stringer.'

'I know who you are Fred. I *said*, "What do you want?"'

'Could you come down and open the door please?'

Too tired to continue with this happy banter, she felt it was easier to go downstairs. Opening the door, she was met by the constable.

'We were worried you had been taken poorly Miss Evans.'

'Who's we?' she asked.

'Well, you know, um, everyone. You haven't picked up your milk, and the papers are on the doorstep.' Looking down, Dolly saw not one but two papers and three pints of milk, two with full cream.

'What day is it Fred?' she asked.

'Wednesday, Miss Evans.'

She opened the door wider for Fred to enter, and he followed her into the kitchen. Telling him to remove his hat – *didn't he have any manners?* – she indicated he should take a seat, and held the kettle under the tap, but for some reason there was no water. 'What's the matter with this thing?' she said.

'I think you'll find you need to turn the tap on first,'

suggested Constable Stringer. Rising from his seat he completed that simple procedure and water flowed, Dolly being unable to hold the kettle and turn the tap due to the cast. Looking around, Constable Stringer saw the bottle of tablets on the counter, and picking them up read the label. 'How many of these have you taken, Miss Evans?' he asked.

'No idea. It said to take one, but what good is one going to do, so I took two at a time.'

This explained the milk and papers on the doorstep, the missing days, and the fact that she had obviously slept in her clothes, her hair looking like she had walked through a hedge backwards. Constable Stringer was relieved to see the bottle now contained the last two tablets, and Miss Evans didn't have gas laid on at the cottage. 'You sit down. I'll make the tea. You realise you've slept for two days?' he said.

Within short order they both were sitting at the kitchen table, Dolly already on her third cup with extra sugar.

'So today's what?'

'Wednesday,' he repeated, raising his eyes to heaven.

'Damn, that means I missed the mobile library and my books are due back.'

'I'll drop them off for you if you like, I'm going into town later. Where are they?' On being told they were beside her bed he went upstairs and collected them, noting that the bed was still made, if somewhat crumpled.

'Miss Evans, will you be lodging a complaint against Mr Milligan or Mr Braithwaite by any chance?' the Constable asked on his return to the kitchen.

'What would I do that for?'

'Well, it was due to Mr Milligan's dog that you fell after all.'

'I never even thought about it, but I WILL NOW!'

Dolly and Constable Stringer finished their tea in companionable silence, and when the time came for him to leave he asked, 'Anything I can do for you before I go?'

'No, I'll be fine, but thanks Fred.' After seeing him out and bolting the door she felt tired, so went back to bed.

The next morning she awoke feeling considerably better but wondering what the smell was. After investigation, she decided it emanated from herself and made her way along the landing to the bathroom. With the water running, she removed her clothes and waited for the bath to fill. Lowering herself with difficulty, and lying back, she relaxed with the heat of the water, the steam rising in clouds. Letting her mind drift, Dolly reached for the washcloth from the rack across the bath, wondering why the cast was so heavy, and looking at it, saw it was starting to disintegrate. Unfortunately nobody at the hospital had thought it necessary to mention it shouldn't be immersed in water. Getting out of the bath and dressing proved a lesson in ingenuity and stamina, but once downstairs, the cast now decidedly soggy, she found herself with no choice but to return to that happy place of healing, and called Dick Chapman, proprietor of the local taxi company.

Back at the hospital, the file from her previous visit recovered, still prominently showing on the front cover a red label warning of an 'Awkward Patient', Dolly waited two hours for the remains of the cast to be removed and a new one applied. The hospital almoner arranged a taxi for the return journey, reminding Dolly to keep the cast dry. By one o'clock she was home, just in time for lunch. She could smell the fish as soon as she walked through the door. While Dolly would eat almost anything, rotten fish was not on the list, and she tossed the packet into the dustbin to the delight of the neighbourhood cats. Opening a tin of baked beans with difficulty and toasting two slices of bread, she felt pleased with herself for accomplishing this relatively simple task, but tired from her morning's adventures she left the dishes and sat in the sitting room, and within minutes was fast asleep.

As Dolly recovered, each day feeling a little better, she thought of Constable Fred Stringer's question; was she going to complain about the fall? Never one to sit quietly when things needed to be done, she convinced herself that she would be doing others a favour – she didn't want the same thing to happen to someone else; besides, she might get some money. She decided to call Constable Stringer. When she said she wished to lodge a complaint against Mr Milligan, she was told Fred would call her back. Later that day the phone rang, and the policeman asked if he and Mr Milligan could come and see her.

'I don't want any trouble Fred,' she said warily.

'There won't be, Miss Evans. I've spoken to him and he feels very badly. He wants to see you and make sure you're all right. We'll be there around five o'clock if that suits you?'

'I suppose so, but I'm not giving him tea, I'll tell you that now.'

At five o'clock on the dot the two men knocked on Dolly's door. Opening it, she saw Bob Milligan standing in front of Constable Stringer. 'Miss Evans, I've come to say how very sorry I am. May I come in?'

Dolly moved back, allowing both of them access, and they followed her into the sitting room. 'When are you going to control that dog of yours?' she said. 'If it wasn't for you I wouldn't be in this mess. I've already had to go and have the cast replaced once. I had to take a taxi there and back and I can't afford all the extra expense, I only have my pension.'

'I'm sorry, Miss Evans, I'm sure you realise I never meant for you to be hurt. How can I make amends?'

'I don't know, it's almost impossible to get anything done with this thing on my arm. I live alone, and I can't even feed myself properly,' said Dolly, warming to her subject and wiping a tear from her eye while sniffling miserably.

'Miss Evans, I understand this is hard for you. Will you allow me to send you on a holiday until you feel better able to cope? All expenses paid of course.'

Constable Stringer, standing behind Mr Milligan, nodded vigorously, silently urging her to accept the offer.

'Well, it would be nice not to have to cook and clean for a while.' Dolly, thinking rapidly, wondered how long she could milk this particular golden cow. 'All right, but I want a decent hotel, not some pokey bed and breakfast.'

'Of course. I'll tell you what, I'll give you five thousand pounds, you can spend it how you like, and that will be the end of it. Do we have a deal?' asked Mr Milligan, holding out his hand.

'Yes,' she said, and shook his hand before he could change his mind, while thinking him a fool. She would have settled for two thousand. He, however, had been prepared to go to ten thousand, and thus they both thought they had the best of the deal. Either way, they both felt good.

'Right, I'm glad that's settled. Mr Milligan will bring a cheque over tomorrow,' said Constable Stringer, and with that they left.

Dolly could hardly believe her good luck. Five thousand pounds! She could do a lot with that, and decided to spend the evening making notes as to how the money could be used to best advantage. After struggling to get a meal, wash and all the minor things that needed to be done with a house, not that she'd admit housekeeping wasn't her first priority, staying at an hotel came out on top, the only decision now being where to go and with whom, for as everyone knew, it was no fun going on holiday by yourself.

The next morning Mr Milligan came by with the cheque, and when Dolly complained she had no way to get to the bank, he insisted on driving her there and waiting for her while she made the deposit. Upon returning to the car she just happened to mention she needed some groceries, so with no choice but to stop at the supermarket and carry all the subsequent purchases, Bob Milligan at last saw Dolly back into her house.

The next couple of days were spent in thought of where she would go for her holiday. She had, before she was asked not to return for disrupting the meetings with her constant interruptions and bickering, been a member of the local women's club, and had attended a slide show last year on the Lake District. It looked so beautiful with the hills and lakes, and after much thought she decided this was the location of choice. The telephone book provided the number of the travel agent in the nearby town of Lower Minchington, and the lady who answered and identified herself as 'Brenda' took the list of requirements. She told Dolly to leave it all up to her, and to expect a call within a couple of days.

With one decision made, another remained. Who should be the lucky one to accompany her? Going through the mental list of her closest friends, she could only think of one who was actually talking to her. Zolanda would be the one on whom she would bestow her good fortune. Zolanda and Dolly had attended school together – recognising in each other a kindred spirit, they had quickly teamed up. Zolanda was teased unmercifully about her name; Dolly about her hair. Her mother, scared of head lice, insisting on a boy's hair cut. As a result, school for both girls was a nightmare, and any opportunity to miss it was grabbed with alacrity, resulting in many happy afternoons spent in detention together.

Dolly phoned the object of her beneficence that evening. After the usual remarks about the weather, the incompetent government, along with the price of beef, Dolly waited impatiently to tell Zolanda her news. At the end of the tale of how she came to be so lucky, making no mention of the amount received, she said, 'And you're coming with me!'

'Who?'

'Are you going deaf? You! You're coming to the Lake District with me. You could at least say thank you.'

'But I'm not sure I want to go there. It's a long way, and I have my night school classes for sewing.'

'Forget the stupid sewing classes, this is an adventure! Did I forget to say I'm paying?'

'When do we leave?' asked Zolanda.

Brenda the travel agent would come to wish she had never answered the phone when Dolly initially called. The poor woman's world was filled with changed arrangements and demands for this or that. Afternoon tea had to be available at the hotel, separate bedrooms were required, each with its own bathroom, it must be within a town, the list went on and on. With arrangements discussed and finalised, confirmations sent by courier to Dolly, the trains reserved, the cars to and from the stations booked – when all was done Brenda booked her own vacation: one week in Bournemouth. Alone.

The day came for their departure. Zolanda had stayed at Dolly's cottage the night before – she knew Dolly's inability to be anywhere at the time stated, and didn't want to risk any problems raising their ugly heads. When she had suggested she stay the night before, Dolly had thought it an excellent idea. With only one bathroom the morning ablutions were somewhat acrimonious, but with looks that could kill and a great deal of loud sighing they were both eventually ready. Zolanda had to help Dolly get dressed, much to their mutual annoyance, but at last, standing by the front door, suitcases at their feet, they waited for the taxi which had been booked for nine o'clock. Dolly asked for the sixth time if Zolanda had locked the back door, and on being told 'yes', went to check for herself.

The troubles started at the train station. The nine-thirty to Manchester was delayed due to signal problems, which now put in jeopardy their connection onward to Morton-Next-the-Sea. Dolly insisted that the station-master present himself to explain the delay but he wisely stayed in his small office, leaving it to the platform guard to deal with her. 'It ain't my fault missus don't yell at me,' he said, and deciding he wasn't paid enough to shoulder the blame, he retreated to the office, banging on the stationmaster's door pleading for admittance. Zolanda sat calmly on a wooden bench underneath an awning, all the kerfuffle passing over her head; she was used to Dolly's temper, it no longer aggrieved her.

'Why are you just sitting there? Can't you say something?' asked Dolly.

'There's hardly any need, you seem to be saying enough for both of us, Dolly.' And once again Zolanda became the very picture of calm. Dolly, her arm in a sling to garner sympathy, paced up and down the platform, and the other five passengers shuffled their way in a group to the end of the platform out of harm's way.

The train arrived fifteen minutes late. If it could make

14

up time they could still make their connection, but the
train gods were not to smile on them that day. As Dolly
had feared, they arrived at Manchester to see the arrivals
and departure board showing the Morton-Next-the-Sea
train being changed to another, whose ultimate desti-
nation was Carlisle. 'Blast the trains,' said Dolly, 'now we
have to wait over an hour.' Along with Zolanda, with an
elderly porter pushing a wagon containing their suitcases
following behind, she marched her way to the station
buffet.

'Let me buy you a nice cup of tea dear,' offered
Zolanda, and before Dolly could find fault with that
suggestion she steered Dolly to a spare table and made
her way to the tea stand. The porter, already grumbling
about the weight he was expected to push, quickly
dumped their cases on the floor beside Dolly's table and
made a run for the staff room, guessing correctly that a
tip would not be forthcoming.

'It doesn't matter, Dolly, you said it would be an adventure and so it is. There's nothing to be done about it
now, why don't you just drink your tea? I bought a nice
currant bun too in case you were hungry,' said Zolanda,
and with no other choice in the matter they both recon-
ciled themselves to the fact that they were marooned at
the station for another hour.

At length, Zolanda went out into the main hall to
check the board for the next train, being unable to
understand the announcements over the public address
system. She came running back into the buffet. 'Hurry
Dolly, there's a train in ten minutes from Platform 4.'
Although they were opposite Platform 1, with no porter
in sight, this shouldn't have posed too large a problem.
However, word had obviously been passed from one
porter to another about the harridan in the buffet, and
they all ensured they were otherwise employed. With two

cases each, and Dolly's broken wrist, the next ten minutes weren't happy ones, and things were said that perhaps would have been better left unsaid, but suffice to say as the guard blew his whistle, and waved his green flag, Dolly threw herself into the carriage behind the suit-cases and Zolanda, landing once more on the floor. With Zolanda's help she managed to right herself, and took a seat as the train glided away from the station. Both were short of breath, and the first five minutes of their journey were spent in silence.

'Well,' said Zolanda, 'that was fun. But we're on our way Dolly!' A fact that couldn't be denied.

A food cart came round after about thirty minutes, but when Dolly found it was three pounds for a ham sand-wich, and told the seller that she had never heard of anything so outrageous, the cart was moved on to richer hunting grounds. Unknown to Dolly, however, and think-ing forward, Zolanda had packed cheese and pickle sand-wiches the night before, each individually wrapped in greaseproof paper. 'Why didn't you say we already had sandwiches?' complained Dolly. 'Why did you allow me to be insulted by that slip of a girl?' Zolanda remembered the exchange differently, but had long ago learned not to contradict her friend. 'I was just interested in how much they were,' she said, and reached into her voluminous carryall. As both now happily munched on their meal, things started to look up.

Brenda the travel agent had no way of knowing of the delay in getting to Morton-Next-the-Sea, and so the taxi driver pre-booked to meet Dolly and Zolanda had given up and gone home for tea. Waiting at last outside the Victorian-era station, they both looked around. A soft drizzle soon began to fall, and they shuffled and pushed their cases back under cover. One taxi came by, stopping to ask where they wanted to go, but on being told The

Eagle Hotel at Grange he looked at their luggage and drove off, leaving Dolly staring after him. 'Well, I hope not everyone is as rude as he,' she said.

Eventually a taxi appeared, a 'people carrier' large enough to hold the two passengers and their luggage, but before their bags were loaded, Dolly asked how much it would cost to be taken to the hotel. 'Ten pounds love,' was the reply. Dolly thought this exorbitant, but with no other conveyance in sight, the drizzle still falling, and the need for a cup of tea uppermost in her mind, she said, 'All right, but don't expect a tip,' thereby endearing herself to the driver, who made sure that he too would be busy should she require transportation again. He offloaded their cases, dumping them on the forecourt of the hotel and, neither knowing nor caring if someone would be coming to help the two old ladies, he drove off. 'It seems everyone here has an attitude problem,' observed Dolly with a loud sniff, and leaving Zolanda guarding the cases, she went into the hotel to find some-one to help with the luggage.

'Sorry madam, we don't have a bellboy,' she was told after requesting assistance. 'I'll see if I can get someone from the dining room to help though,' and the recep-tionist bustled off. Dolly drummed her fingers on the counter. This wasn't exactly going the way she had planned, and the sling for her wrist wasn't having quite the effect she had hoped, but putting it down to bad manners she waited for that 'someone'.

Zolanda meanwhile remained with the cases in the rain, and having given up waiting for help was moving them herself one by one to shelter. An Italian waiter by the name of Giuseppe eventually came to their rescue, picking up two cases at once as if they were feathers. Enquiring for their room numbers from the reception-ist, Dolly's was 305, Zolanda's 307, he took their

17

respective keys and sped up the stairs. In the absence of a lift, Dolly and Zolanda trailed behind, both puffing after one floor, gasping by two, and almost on their knees by the third. 'I'm going to kill that Brenda when I get back. Why didn't she book a hotel with a lift?' asked Dolly of no one in particular when she had regained the power of speech. Zolanda, too breathless, was unable to answer.

By six o'clock in the evening they were both unpacked, rooms organised to their requirements. Both rooms overlooked the sea, though Dolly privately thought Zolanda's should have been a 'garden view' since she hadn't actually paid. Feeling magnanimous, she decided not to cause a fuss. The rooms were large and sunny, with plenty of storage space. The beds looked (and felt) comfortable, though personally Dolly wasn't partial to the modern fashion for duvets, preferring an old-fashioned counterpane. However, trying to think positively, she was determined to enjoy herself. Dressed for dinner, she had arranged to meet Zolanda outside the dining room at six-fifteen, and again wearing the sling to ensure no one would miss the cast on her arm, she set off downstairs.

2

Dolly's instructions to Brenda had, she thought, been quite clear. A small hotel, set within the town confines, two bedrooms, each with a bathroom – all this had been fulfilled, but there it ended. As registered guests, Dolly thought a table should have been reserved for them automatically. However, when they presented themselves at the dining room door it was to find that half of the tables were already occupied, the other half cordoned off as the ceiling above had been leaking from the rain, which apparently had been non-stop for the past two days. Tired and hungry, they were both disappointed to be told they should take a seat in the bar, 'Someone will come and get you when we have a table free.' Dolly was left speechless, an occurrence so rare that Zolanda felt compelled to take her diary out and make a note of this momentous event.

'What are you doing?' hissed Dolly.

'Making a note that you're speechless,' Zolanda replied.

'Don't you dare or I'll send you home on the next train.'

'No you won't, you can't get dressed without me.'

They decided to take a seat at the bar, but as neither could climb up on the bar stools they retreated to a table with four chairs. The Italian waiter who had taken their bags to their rooms came in, and Dolly waved a finger at him, which he duly ignored. 'Hoi, didn't you see me wave at you? We want a drink over here,' she called out.

'I'll get the barman to help you,' he replied, and wandered off through a swing door marked 'Private'. They waited some five minutes but nobody else appeared, until Dolly could stand it no longer. Deciding if no one would get a drink for them she would do it herself, she went over to the bar, lifted the flap in the counter with her good hand and walked behind it.

'What do you fancy Zolanda?'

'Red wine I think.'

Dolly looked around for a bottle of wine. It was amazing how different it looked from this side of the counter, so many bottles and glasses that she felt quite confused. Hunting around and opening cupboards, she opened a small fridge standing on the floor. As she was rummaging inside, giving a running commentary to Zolanda in case anything other than wine took her fancy, a stentorian voice made her jump. 'What the hell do you think you're doing?' it asked. As Dolly jumped, she raised her head and hit her forehead on the optic containing gin.

'What the hell?' she said. Slowly appearing over the counter she saw an extremely angry face looking back at her. This must be the barman. 'Well, we waited long enough for you to come. Is this the way to treat guests in the hotel?' She had decided attack was the best defence.

'You're not allowed behind the bar, come on out,' he said, and Dolly shuffled out, making sure he saw her sling, and holding her bleeding forehead with her good hand.

'Come here Dolly, I've got some tissues in my purse,' said Zolanda, ready to tend to the injured forehead.

'What was it you wanted?' asked the barman.

'Two glasses of wine. Red wine. And not the rubbish you no doubt normally serve, we want something decent,' said Dolly, pushing away Zolanda's ministering hand, which was buzzing around her head like an extremely irritating fly. As can be imagined, the barman made no great hurry in fulfilling the order as stated. As he slowly came from behind the bar carrying two glasses of red wine the waitress from the dining room appeared and said, 'Are you the two women who wanted a table for dinner?'

'No, we are the two *guests* who *requested* a table for dinner,' replied Dolly, and picking up her glass of wine she told the barman to add it to the bill, Room 305. Leaving Zolanda to follow, she sailed behind the waitress to their table, blood still trickling down her forehead.

Perusing the menu, Dolly held a tissue to her head. The first page showed starters and salads, the second entrees, the third desserts. She always looked at the desserts first, the choices held therein helping to make her decisions from pages one and two. 'What are you having?' asked Zolanda.

'I've just opened the menu, Zolanda,' Dolly replied. 'Give me a minute,' and she sat back, prepared to examine each offering at length. This worked out well, until they both realised at the same time that it had been some fifteen minutes since they had been seated and they had not seen the waitress again. Dolly looked around and saw people at other tables looking around, she presumed also for the waitress. As there only seemed to be the one person on duty, either she was in the kitchen getting someone's food, or she had gone home. Dolly decided that it was the latter, and got up and went to the door she presumed led through to the kitchen. It was painted black with a round window at the top. She looked through, but there wasn't a soul in sight. There was a great deal of food on the counter, but no sign of anyone at all. As she put her hand out to push the door, watched not only by Zolanda but also by the rest of the inhabitants of the dining room, the door swung open, hitting her smack on the nose. It appeared she had been standing in front of the 'Out' door rather than the 'In' door. She felt the crunch of the bone, and knew immediately she was in trouble.

As she sat with Zolanda in the hospital emergency room holding a wad of tissues to her nose, she said, 'I don't believe it.'

'Sorry, what did you say?'

'I *said*, I don't believe it. Would you look up and see if there's a black cloud over my head? It hurts to move, but I'm sure it's there, there's no other explanation for all these accidents. Either that or someone is trying to have me killed,' Dolly said, feeling very sorry for herself.

'Well, Dolly, you do get yourself into some messes don't you?'

'It wasn't my fault the door opened out instead of in, how was I to know?'

They had waited for over an hour to see a doctor, and when Dolly was eventually called she wasn't in the best of humour. 'What happened to you?' asked the doctor. 'Been in a fight?'

That was a little too close to the truth for Dolly, and she gave him a withering look. Not being a stupid man, well he wouldn't be would he, being a doctor, he realised she didn't have a very good sense of humour, and immediately set to fixing the broken appendage.

After an extremely painful time, Dolly came out to meet up again with Zolanda. Her nose covered with a large plaster, her eyes black and blue, she felt pretty glum. 'Oh dear,' said Zolanda. 'You look pretty awful Dolly. Do you feel all right?' Dolly just looked at her. The doctor, while he had a captive audience, had also put a butterfly sticking plaster on the cut on her forehead, so with her broken arm (still in the sling), the sticking plaster on her head and the broken nose, she wouldn't have won any beauty prizes. It was late, and they still hadn't had dinner – Zolanda hadn't had the nerve to find the cafeteria while she waited for Dolly in case she should suddenly appear.

Outside, where during the day there would have been a row of taxis, there was but one, and the driver watched them making their way carefully towards him. It took a few minutes as he was parked some distance away, but he stood outside the cab waiting for them. 'I suppose it was too much to expect you could have moved this thing when you saw me struggling over, wasn't it?' said Dolly to the driver as Zolanda assisted her into the back. Raising his eyes to heaven and wishing he could be anywhere but here, he asked where they wanted to go, and upon being told threw the car into first gear and roared away. As they turned into the main road from the hospital driveway Zolanda and Dolly were thrown into one corner, at which point Dolly had had enough and burst into tears – but stopped abruptly when she realised if she continued this particular form of self pity she would have to blow her nose.

Back at the hotel once more, they found the kitchen now closed and the bar locked, and they were left with no other choice but to retire to their rooms. After Zolanda had helped Dolly get ready for bed, a trying time for both, Zolanda retired at last. Lying in bed and picking up her library book, too wound up to go to sleep, she suddenly remembered she had an emergency stash of two chocolate bars in her suitcase, and after finding them and returning to bed, lay back happily munching her supper. *Life doesn't get much better than this,* she thought, plumping up the pillows.

The next morning, dressed and ready for whatever the day would bring, Zolanda tentatively knocked on Dolly's door.

'What!' shouted Dolly.

'Are you all right? Do you want to get up and dressed? What about breakfast?'

'That's three things, Zolanda. I can't think of all that at once. Come in, the door's open.'

As Zolanda stuck her head round the door, Dolly added, 'In fact it's been open for over two hours waiting for you to come and help me. There wasn't much point in you coming on holiday if you're not going to help, was there?'

Zolanda closed the door behind her and looked at her friend, for friend she was. Her eyes were black from the broken nose, the dried blood was still crusted around the cut in her forehead, and her fingers looked like black sausages, swollen and painful. 'I've been trapped here waiting for you to turn up, I'm dying to go to the bathroom,' Dolly said, trying to wriggle her way out of bed.

'Just wait a minute Dolly, I'll help.' Zolanda levered her out of bed and held the bathroom door open for her.

Dolly would have loved a bath but it all seemed too much effort. She remembered with a shiver what she now thought of as 'The Episode of the Soggy Cast' and didn't want to end up back at the hospital, albeit a Lake District hospital, so decided a good wash would have to suffice. Easier said than done. It took a while before she called Zolanda to come and help her dress. By the time they had made their way down to the dining room Dolly was thinking that it might have been better to have had room service, should such a thing be available in this establishment, but she soldiered on, if only for Zolanda's sake. The breakfast service was just coming to an end, but she appeared to be an object of some interest to the staff who kept poking their heads round the 'Out' door of the kitchen to look at her. A different waitress from last night deigned to make coffee and toast for them, 'even though breakfast finishes at nine o'clock'. Zolanda looked at her watch. It was five minutes past, which didn't bode well for the rest of their stay.

It was a silent meal. Dolly saw an abandoned paper on a nearby table and sent Zolanda over to get it. As it had been her idea she insisted on reading it first, leaving Zolanda to look at the back page which contained only the sports scores. She decided to spend the time while she waited for Dolly to finish thinking of what they would do today – she was eager to get out, and with the sun shining she felt it would be a good idea to walk around the town. But as with most things, it all depended on Dolly. Coffee and toast partaken, Dolly felt more able to converse, and asked Zolanda what she would like to do.

'I rather fancied a walk around the town, to get our bearings. What do you want to do?'

'I suppose that would be all right, it depends on the weather forecast of course. We'll ask at the desk on our way upstairs.'

Breakfast over, they made their way to the reception desk. A young man wearing a lounge suit and bright red tie looked up from the computer screen at their approach.

'Good morning ladies, how can I help?'

'Well, this makes a change,' said Dolly. 'Everybody else who works in this hotel seems not to understand the principle of customer service. What's the weather going to do today?'

The young man, wearing a badge proclaiming him the proud possessor of the name Trevor, looked back at the computer, and soon had the information to hand.

'Rain later this afternoon, but sunny this morning,' he said.

Zolanda looked at Dolly. 'Good, that's means we can go for a walk around town.' Thanking Trevor, she and Dolly made their way up the three flights of stairs to their respective rooms to prepare themselves for the outing. Dolly arrived back downstairs some twenty minutes later, complete with raincoat over her good arm. 'You won't need that, Dolly, he said rain this afternoon, it's only ten o'clock, we've plenty of time,' admonished Zolanda. She turned to look at Trevor, who was gazing back at them – it seemed he had heard this exchange, and was nodding his head in agreement.

'Oh very well,' said Dolly, and walking over to the desk said, 'I'll leave it here. Have it taken to my room young man.' She threw the coat on the counter and followed Zolanda out of the front door.

The Eagle Hotel, handily situated in the centre of Morton, faced the sea. A small, granite-built edifice, it consisted of turrets and towers with the obligatory resplendent gargoyles, and on the left-hand side what looked like crenellated battlements, which Dolly thought made the whole place look to have aspirations beyond its ability. A paved forecourt allowed parking for guests coming and going, and the large double glass doors into the reception area were flanked by tubs of tired-looking geraniums and alyssum doing their best to welcome everyone through the doors, but failing miserably.

Turning left at the pavement, they stood for a moment looking out over the sea – the tide was out so it took a little imagination – and both taking deep lungfuls of fresh sea air, they set off. The sky, a pale blue but with just a few fluffy clouds, promised a delightful walk as they explored everything the town had to offer. Dolly was privately glad she hadn't brought the raincoat with her;

what with her handbag and the arm in the sling she had enough to contend with. Zolanda oohed and aahed her way along, stopping every two minutes to admire a garden or the sea view, and Dolly began to think they would never get anywhere. Their journey took them towards a park on the edge of the sea, in the middle of which stood a beautiful bandstand. A sign tacked on one of the pillars proclaimed that next Sunday at two o'clock in the afternoon the brass band would be playing for everyone's enjoyment. Tea and cake would also be available at a nominal price (cash only accepted) for those wishing to partake of some refreshment. 'We must come to that,' said Zolanda. 'It's been years since I've listened to a brass band, it'll be fun Dolly, you'll see,' she went on, looking anxiously at Dolly's face.

As they moved past the bandstand, Zolanda looked at the sky. There were certainly more clouds gathering, some of them quite dark. But Trevor had said no rain until the afternoon, and being a positive thinker she hoped that Dolly wasn't aware of the gathering storm. Unfortunately they had walked past the bandstand by some five minutes when Zolanda felt the first drops. Dolly, who was plodding along staring at the pavement to ensure she didn't trip over anything, didn't seem to have noticed. 'Shall we turn back now Dolly?' Zolanda said.

'Why? You're the one who wanted to explore.'

'Yes, I know, but I think it might be about to rain.'

Dolly looked up at the sky, two raindrops landing on her face. From the sky she looked around, but there was no shelter. They couldn't even see the top of the bandstand roof from where they were. There were trees, but Zolanda had this fear of standing under trees; you never knew when a storm would become thunder and lightning.

'We'll have to get a move on,' said Zolanda, and

lengthened her stride, heading back to the bandstand.

'I distinctly remember I wanted to bring my raincoat, Zolanda. You and that awful little creature Trevor advised me I wouldn't need it. Do you remember that Zolanda?'

'Of course I do Dolly, but being in another bad mood isn't going to help. Just hurry up.'

The rain was now falling steadily, and they walked as fast as they could along the path. Dolly was very worried about her cast and tried to shelter it underneath her cardigan. As the rain became heavier it soon became apparent that she would have to remove the cardigan and wrap it around her arm. Still hurrying as much as she could, she asked Zolanda to hold her handbag. It had been difficult in the hotel getting the sleeve over the cast, and it was even harder to remove the sleeve while hurrying along, getting wetter by the moment. 'There it is, there's the bandstand,' said Zolanda, and put on a final spurt to reach shelter. Dolly meanwhile had had to stand still to remove the cardigan, and once she had done that had wrapped it, mummy-like, around the cast, which to her now felt suspiciously spongy.

At last they reached shelter. With the absence of seats of any kind, they were forced to stand in the middle beneath the roof's high pitch, the rain coming sideways from the west. Zolanda held her breath, waiting for the explosion that was bound to come.

'Bloody hell Zolanda, what a stupid idea. I should have listened to my intuition and stayed inside. I'm absolutely soaked, and heaven knows what's happening to this cast. The woman at the hospital told me not to get it wet, and now look at it,' Dolly said, unwinding the now soggy cardigan to reveal one very soggy cast.

'Oh dear Dolly, it looks like it will have to be replaced. You don't seem to be having much luck do you?'

For once Dolly managed to maintain control and just

stood silently. But if only Zolanda had known what she was thinking.

They walked back into the hotel wet through. Before Dolly could go once again to the hospital, they both had to change into something dry. Pausing on each landing to regain their breath, they eventually came to the third floor. Zolanda accompanied Dolly into her room to help her change, and then returned to her own room to do the same. Meeting outside in the hall, they went back downstairs and asked the girl working at reception to call a taxi. Upon being told one would be outside in five minutes, they decided to wait in the lobby, the rain having stopped and the sun now shining. Opening the doors, Zolanda said, 'It smells so lovely outside, Dolly, the rain makes everything smell so nice. Let's wait outside.' Dolly, acquiescent for once, followed her out. A taxi came onto the forecourt, coincidentally the same driver who had delivered them to the establishment on their arrival, the one who had been told not to expect a tip. Seeing the two standing there, he drove round in a circle and went out again.

Zolanda, quick on the uptake, went back into reception and asked for another taxi to be called, and thirty minutes later they were on their way to the hospital.

At the nurses' station Dolly explained the problem, and the nurse told them to take a seat and someone would be with them shortly. The 'shortly' turned out to be an hour later, by which time Dolly was almost apoplectic. She had been back to the desk twice to ask what the hold up was. Upon being told emergencies were dealt with before soggy casts, she demanded to see the hospital administrator. As nothing was going to come of that she returned to sit beside Zolanda, who had spent a very happy hour reading a ladies' magazine giving some very timely information on 'How to Deal with Toxic Friends'.

'Can I get you a cup of tea or coffee?' she asked Dolly.

'No, if I drink any more I'll have to keep going to the toilet, and I can guarantee as soon as I leave this seat someone will come and call my name, I'm not taking any chances,' and she sat resolute.

'Well, I think I'll get something, I'm a little peckish.' Zolanda left Dolly, following the signs for the cafeteria.

'Dolly Evans?' called a young man holding a stack of papers in his hand and looking inquisitively around the waiting room.

'That's me,' she said, holding up her good hand.

'Come with me,' and he set off down the corridor at a rate of speed that was impossible for Dolly to match.

'Hoi, wait for me. Why the hell are you walking so quickly?' She glowered at him as he turned and waited for her, making irritating 'hurry up' gestures with his hand. Opening a door for her, he told her to take a seat, and said that someone would be with her shortly.

A young girl appeared from yet another door and looked at Dolly. 'So what's the problem?' she asked. She was dressed all in white – Dolly presumed that was to make her seem clean and professional. She had long wavy red hair and was wearing white shoes. In Dolly's estimation she was about fifteen years old, but if she worked here she had to be older.

'Well, as you can see, the cast got wet and has gone all soggy.'

'Didn't anyone tell you not to get it wet?'

'Well yes, but I was caught out in the rain this morning and well, it got wet.'

Tutting and sighing, the girl took a little buzz saw and ran it up Dolly's arm. 'What colour do you want?' she asked.

'Huh?' asked Dolly, uncomprehendingly.

'Yes, colour. Red, pink, green, blue or white? Take your

pick, but hurry up about it, you're not the only person here you know.'

Dolly, instantly alert, realised that here was another person who had missed the 'bedside manner' class. 'Pink,' she replied.

The new cast applied, she then had to go for yet another X-ray to ensure the bone was set properly. All this took time, of course, and Dolly had long since run out of patience. At last she made her weary way back to the waiting room to find Zolanda drinking tea and munching a sandwich.

'Oh, are you finished? Do you want something to eat now Dolly? They have some very nice sandwiches I must say.'

'No, I just want to go back and lie down, I feel proper poorly.'

Zolanda looked at her friend – indeed she did look proper poorly. The parts of her face that weren't black and blue and covered with sticking plaster, or red from the cut, looked very downcast.

'Come on Dolly, let's go.' Taking Dolly's good arm, Zolanda led her gently outside. Back at the hotel the walk up the three flights of stairs totally finished Dolly off, and she retired to bed for the rest of the day, telling Zolanda not to disturb her.

Zolanda, in her second-best dress and wearing her new white shawl, presented herself at the dining room door. As if by magic a table was available for her, the waitress instantly at her side offering bread and a drink of choice, presenting the menu and generally being an all round 'good egg'. *This is the life* Zolanda thought, merrily signing the bill to Dolly's account.

The next morning dawned bright and sunny. Dolly awoke at seven o'clock feeling refreshed and eager to get on with the holiday. As had become their routine, Zolanda helped her dress, and together they descended to the dining room. Not having dined the night before, Dolly ordered the Full English Breakfast, including the black pudding (double order) and fried bread. 'Might as well be hung for a sheep as a lamb,' she reasoned, and added to the order two slices of brown toast. With butter.

Zolanda, who it will be recalled had partaken of a wonderful dinner, ordered half a grapefruit with toast and coffee. The weather forecast – this time they had checked for themselves on the televisions in their rooms – showed clear skies for the next two days, and Dolly, feeling so much better, suggested a trip to the nearby town of Kendal. Now Zolanda hadn't come to the Lake District to go shopping, she had come for the lakes and fells, and the suggestion fell on an unhappy face.

'What's the matter Zolanda? Don't you want to go shopping?'

'No I don't, I can do that at home thank you very much. Let's go out into the countryside instead.'

'We can do that at home too. No, I think it'll be Kendal today, we can go on the bus. Think of it as an adventure, Zolanda. You really must try not to be so negative all the time.' And she addressed herself to the large platter placed before her by the waitress with, she thought, unnecessary force.

Dolly had never been the owner of a sylphlike figure, and try though she might she seemed unable to lose weight. Diet after diet had been tried and, with no result, been discarded, and she had come to accept that she would always be pleasantly plump. Lately however, the pleasantly plump had morphed into just plain fat, but looking in the mirror she saw herself as slim and attractive. Unfortunately she still wore the same clothes as when she was pleasantly plump, but now even she could tell changes had to be made. She intended looking for some new clothes in Kendal.

They made enquiries at reception. The bus to Kendal stopped outside the train station, being the most convenient location, so they decided on the ten-fifty, which would get them to Kendal by eleven twenty-five. There was time enough before that to enjoy the morning, and again reserving a taxi for their trip to the station they looked forward to their day. For once the taxi was on time, they arrived at the bus stop with five minutes to spare, the bus arrived with plenty of seats, and they settled back to enjoy the journey, Dolly exclaiming, 'This is such fun!'

The next stop was at the next village, where a lady carrying a canary in a cage stood waiting. The bus driver addressed her by name, leaping from his seat to assist her by taking the cage and helping her to a seat, placing the canary next to her. Obviously she and her canary were well known to everyone. She looked around, greeting other passengers by name until her gaze rested on Dolly and Zolanda. 'Good morning,' she said. Zolanda acknowledged her with the same greeting. Dolly sat looking out of the window. At last the bus was on its way again.

No sooner had the bus moved off than the canary began to sing. Now everybody likes a canary, they're such bright cheery creatures, their song happy and uplifting. How could one fail to be encouraged by their demeanour? It was just unfortunate that Dolly was on that particular bus, for within a very short time of listening to the aforementioned happy song she thought she would go mad. 'What time does this stupid bus get to Kendal?' she asked Zolanda.

'Eleven twenty-five, another half an hour,' she replied, checking her watch.

'Holy Hannah, do we have to put up with this all that time? Why doesn't she shut it up?' While the bus as it laboured along was noisy, Dolly's voice was of such a timbre that it could be heard above the grinding of gears. Zolanda was aware of the other passengers glaring at them, and she wanted to scream, 'It's her, not me!' She wisely kept her counsel, however, and followed Dolly by looking out of the window. The countryside was wonderful. Woolly sheep dotted the fields which were green and lush, quaint stone buildings some with thatched roofs sped by, but all Zolanda wanted to do was to sink beneath the seat.

The next half hour was spent in exquisite torture, on the one hand listening to the happy tra-las of the canary, on the other, sitting next to Dolly. To the relief of everyone the bus eventually ground its way into Kendal, stopping at the bus station. The lady with the canary sat still, waiting for the bus to empty before getting off herself, along with the canary. As Dolly passed down the narrow aisle, she had to turn sideways due to her girth. She stopped by the lady. 'Madam, why did you bring that bird on the bus?' she asked.

'I always bring Chippy on the bus, she loves the ride.'

Unable to think of a reply to do the remark justice, Dolly struggled down the steps, followed by Zolanda. 'Have you ever heard anything like it?' she asked. 'Why would that silly woman bring a canary shopping with her?' Dolly looked around, and without asking which way to the shops, set forth.

Zolanda looked behind her. The lady with the canary was waiting by the side of the path, two small children running over to her. 'Grandma, you're here,' they said, huge smiles on their small faces. They both kissed the old lady then turned their attention to the birdcage, talking to Chippy as if the bird were a person. A younger lady came up and put her arm round the lady with the cage, kissing her on the cheek then leading her away to a waiting car. *What a lovely little family,* thought Zolanda, who had never had a family of her own.

She had been married when she was twenty-three to a man she had met at the local Conservative meeting. He was tall and dark with excellent prospects within the bank for which he worked, and Zolanda had quickly fallen head over heels in love. Within a year they were married. Within another year she knew she had made a terrible mistake, finding lipstick on handkerchiefs, the smell of perfume on his clothes. When confronted, he admitted to affairs and readily agreed to a divorce. From falling in love to divorce took three years, and Zolanda had been alone now for over forty years. She had never met anyone else with whom she wished to spend those years, content with the life she had been given. Luckily, or unluckily depending upon her mood, children had never arrived but now, watching the little family, she felt sad.

'Will you come *on*, Zolanda,' shouted Dolly. 'We don't have all day.' Zolanda turned slowly and followed.

Kendal, a market town nestled amongst the hills, was very busy and within short order they both felt in need of a cup of tea. A small café along the High Street soon came into view, and in they went. Not a large place, it seemed friendly. Asking for two teas and a scone with cream each, Zolanda found an empty table. The tea and scones duly arrived, and they sat in companionable silence looking out of the window as the rest of the world rushed by. Feeling better for the sit down, they paid, then visited shop after shop, Zolanda enjoying the hustle and bustle, Dolly looking for new clothes, and as usual complaining about the noise, the crowds, the walking. By four o'clock they had both had enough, and with Dolly emptyhanded in the clothes department, made their way back to the bus station in time to catch the four-thirty bus. Having bought return tickets they didn't have to queue at the ticket office. They asked where to get the Grange bus and, being directed over to the right, they looked at a long line snaking its way down the pavement.

'Oh lord,' said Zolanda, 'I hope they aren't all waiting for the same bus as us.' But this proved to be the case and after joining the end of the queue, Dolly voiced her feelings. 'All I know is I'm getting on this bus no matter what.' Once again Zolanda tried to look as if they weren't together. With the appearance of the bus, the general push and shove commenced, Dolly holding up her pink cast in case anyone should hit it, while at the same time using it as a battering ram. Hauling Zolanda after her, she found two seats right at the back, and thankfully they sat down, each long ago wishing they had worn more comfortable shoes. Looking out of the window as they left the bus station, Dolly totally ignored those who had been in front of them in the queue, her motto for this week being 'In this life, one has to look after oneself'.

Back at the hotel both needed a rest before dinner, but the rest turned into more of a nap, and it was seven o'clock before they were assembled at the dining room door. 'You'll have to wait in the bar, there's no room,' they were again told, and Zolanda quickly steered Dolly towards the now familiar bar.

'Why don't they fix the damn roof, how difficult can it be?' Dolly asked. 'That Brenda person is going to get the sharp edge of my tongue when I get home let me tell you.' She sat down with a thud in a chair. To the minute of half an hour of waiting they were told a table was available, and following the waitress in and taking their seats, they found the tablecloth dirty from the previous occupants. But Dolly, even after her nap, was too beaten down with tiredness to complain. Choosing from the menu, she found her first two choices were no longer available. 'You are late you know,' she was told, and settled for the lamb chops. Zolanda chose shepherd's pie. Both too weary to talk, they sat in silence. Declining dessert and coffee they made their weary way upstairs in stages, like deep sea divers who have to decompress every so many feet, and fell into their beds, another day behind them.

3

Of the five nights booked at The Eagle Hotel, two had now passed. The third day, Sunday, they awoke to rain. Not just ordinary rain, but torrential rain. At breakfast the area cordoned off in the dining room was still out of bounds, but now sported cheerful pails and containers of all sizes and colours, two on tables, the rest on the floor, catching what appeared to be small rivers from the roof. 'When is someone going to do something about that?' enquired Dolly of the waitress at breakfast.

'Well, they can't do anything about while it's raining can they?' was the reply.

'But it's been like that since we arrived two days ago, and the sun has shone some of the time.'

'It's none of my business,' said the waitress, bustling off to the kitchen to give their order. Looking to the entrance to the dining room, Dolly could see faces peering round the door looking for a table, but she didn't feel any pity; all she knew was that she was sitting down and about to be fed. Everyone for himself in this world. Woken from this reverie, she realised Zolanda was speaking.

'Dolly, what are we going to do today?'

'How the hell do I know? Why do I have to make all the decisions?'

'Well, I did suggest a trip to the countryside if you remember, but you wanted to go shopping instead.'

'Well, we can't go to the countryside today, can we

Zolanda? Not in this monsoon. It looks like we'll have to stay here until it stops, whenever that is.' Dolly, never one to go looking for things to do, was looking forward to staying inside. Looking at the rain beating against the window, then glancing at the happy pink cast on her arm, she knew outside was a place she definitely didn't want to be. No more hospitals for her, she had used up her quota as far as she was concerned. Besides, today was the first day she felt anything like normal, or as normal as Dolly ever felt and she didn't want to do anything to jeopardise that. Refusing to hurry her meal, she could feel accusing eyes upon her, glaring at her actually to hurry and free up the table, but she had every intention of enjoying the morning. As another table cleared, and the accusing eyes walked past their table, she was aware of the glares but as usual just didn't care.

By ten o'clock the rain had lessened to a steady downpour, by eleven to a shower, and by one o'clock the sun was shining. Having eaten a large breakfast, and not interested in lunch just yet, they decided to go out. No longer taking Trevor's word for anything, they took their raincoats this time and wandered away from the hotel. Dolly, by now used to her black and blue face, ignored the stares as they progressed, and for once, both friends enjoyed themselves at the same time. Morton-Next-the-Sea, though not large, offered a good variety of shops, and the seafront had plenty of sitting areas, but it wasn't until they again came upon their shelter in the storm, the bandstand, that they remembered the concert was due to begin at two o'clock. Already most of the deckchairs were taken, and the grass around the bandstand had a few occupants wisely encamped on waterproof sheets. 'Dolly, can we listen to the band do you think?' asked Zolanda tentatively.

Dolly, for once in the land of 'all is right with the world', answered, 'Of course, if you would like to,' and moving swiftly just beat an elderly man and woman, both walking with canes, to the last-remaining deckchairs. Totally ignoring their looks of disgust she said, 'Go and see if the tea thingy is open, Zolanda, I fancy a cuppa and a piece of cake.' Placing her raincoat on the ground beside her, she leaned back and raised her face to the sun.

The tea thingy was indeed open, and Zolanda, upon ordering two teas both with milk and sugar and two pieces of coffee and walnut cake for a very reasonable price, was given a tray on which to carry everything and carefully made her way back to Dolly. She could hear quite quickly that Dolly had fallen asleep, for it was the snoring that gave it away. Blissfully oblivious, Dolly slept on while the band in their smart military-style uniforms assembled, tuned their respective instruments, announced the offerings of the day and began to play. Zolanda enjoyed the two cups of tea and two slices of coffee and walnut cake, and herself dozed, replete.

It must have been the lack of noise that woke Dolly. Coming awake with a start, she found they were alone but for a lady walking a particularly ugly little dog, and a man with a long stick and a point on the end picking up litter. 'Wassa time?' asked Dolly, slowly coming out of her coma.

'It's four o'clock Dolly, and you've slept all through the concert,' said Zolanda, annoyance for once quite clear in her voice.

'So why didn't you wake me?'

'I don't think that would have been a good idea, do you? You're never at your best when you first wake up, are you?' This couldn't be denied, so Dolly didn't even bother.

The thing about deckchairs is how nice they look, with their cheerful striped seating, the way the breeze blows the fabric, so very reminiscent of sunny British seaside holiday postcards, row upon row of them waiting for pasty-skinned occupants, beckoning 'come, sit down, rest your weary bones'. They always look so inviting, until you try and leave them. Then they turn vicious, not providing enough leverage to haul the aforementioned weary bones from their embrace. Invariably it ends up with too much skin being revealed as you struggle and groan your way upright.

Zolanda, being slimmer and more agile than Dolly, managed without too much difficulty. But now it was Dolly's turn. The task was made even more entertaining as, for those of us who have forgotten, Dolly was sporting a cast. With two healthy hands the task is difficult; with one it is nigh-on impossible. Dolly's language, never pure, became even less so. Zolanda tried hauling her up by standing behind and placing her hands under Dolly's arms, but was pulled forwards instead. She stood to the left of Dolly, hauling on her good arm, but that didn't work either. Then she had the answer. Zolanda would just tip the deckchair over so Dolly would be able to release herself. The lady with the dog and the man with the pointed stick had disappeared to pastures greener, and after consulting with Dolly who reluctantly agreed, as she herself could see no other way, Zolanda pushed and shoved. The deckchair made ominous creaking noises, eventually tipping onto its side.

Dolly was lying on the ground. Unfortunately as she had sat down, then settled further into the chair as she slept, her skirt had crept up at the back. Neither combatant realised this until Zolanda, removing the chair, was greeted with the sight of Dolly's bright-blue knickers on full view to any who cared, or indeed were brave enough, to look. She hastily adjusted Dolly's skirt and decided, wisely, not to mention the occurrence, watching while Dolly turned herself right side up like a large black beetle. Slowly but surely, Dolly came first to her knees, then with Zolanda's help she stood five foot three tall once more. 'Bloody hell Zolanda, I could do with a cup of tea.'

Neither made any further comment about this embarrassing episode as they headed back to their hotel. However, Zolanda couldn't help thinking, and rightly so, that if Dolly hadn't been so rude as to take the deckchairs from the elderly couple in the first place, the whole thing could well have been avoided.

Opting for the later sitting for dinner, which began at eight o'clock, they went to their rooms. Zolanda read her library book. Dolly ordered a cup of tea from room service, but was not best pleased to be presented in due course with a tray on which reposed a cup and saucer, a tiny pot of hot water, tea bag leaning against its side, pre-packed milk and a bag of sugar. *How long can I realistically bear this awful place?* she thought. Arriving at the dining room at eight o'clock on the dot, they found their table not quite ready. Dolly refused to go to the bar to wait and stood four-square in the doorway glaring at anyone brave enough to look her way. Thus it was after ten when their meal was over, Zolanda spending most of the time covering yawns with her hand. Dolly said, 'I don't know why you keep yawning Zolanda, it's very bad manners in case you've forgotten.' But Zolanda was past caring. Hardly able to wait for the coffee, which she didn't even want, to arrive, she gulped it down, gathered her purse and shawl from the floor beside her, stood up and said, 'I'm going to bed Dolly, I'm very tired.'

Dolly looked at her. 'But how am I going to get undressed?'

'To be honest Dolly, I neither know nor care.' And with that, Zolanda left Dolly looking at her rapidly retreating back.

Monday dawned a beautiful day. Zolanda woke refreshed and, she had to admit, rather pleased with herself for the way she had stood up to Dolly. 'I really must do that more often,' she thought. Smiling at herself in the mirror as she brushed her hair, she told herself to continue with this assertive mood throughout the day. As soon as she knocked on Dolly's door, however, she knew she was in trouble. Dolly was obviously upset with her, and already she felt her resolve slipping away. 'Good morning Dolly, how are you today?'

Silence.

'Dolly, I asked how you were today?'

Silence.

'Well, if you aren't talking to me, I'm going downstairs,' and she made for the bedroom door.

'Where are you going?' asked Dolly.

'I said good morning twice and you ignored me, so I'm going downstairs for breakfast.'

'And how do you expect me to dress myself? It was bad enough trying to get undressed, I don't want to go through that again, so get out of this bad mood you appear to be in.'

Zolanda looked at her, hardly believing her ears. *She* was in a bad mood? Dolly seemed to spend her life in a bad mood, and it was Zolanda who usually bore the brunt of it. Then she remembered Dolly was paying for the holiday and, feeling guilty, said, 'All right Dolly, I'll help.'

'What's the plan for today?' asked Dolly, buttering her third piece of brown toast.

'What would you like to do, Dolly?'

'I was thinking, how about a trip to Lake Windermere? We could take one of those cruises that are advertised. What would you say to that?'

'Oh Dolly, that would be wonderful! It will be such fun, and the day looks glorious too. But are you sure Dolly? It could be expensive?'

'Oh that's all right, we deserve a nice day,' and with that, the decision was made. A tour bus came by the hotel at ten-thirty, space reserved for them both by the girl at the reception desk. Upstairs they gathered everything they thought they might need, and for the first time since their arrival Zolanda took her camera. As they waited in the lobby for the bus they both felt quite excited. Dolly had packed a small bag, which Zolanda would have to carry, but that wasn't a problem, or it wasn't a problem for Dolly, and it was with great anticipation they watched the twelve-seater drive onto the forecourt.

'Two for Windermere?' asked the driver through the window. 'That's us,' said Dolly, and she and Zolanda climbed aboard. There were eight other occupants, obviously picked up at previous stops, spread around the bus, however there weren't two seats together. Instantly recognising this fact, Dolly settled on a victim. 'You, move over there, my friend and I want to sit together.' She seemed to have no doubt that the instructions would be obeyed, and indeed they were, the poor man scurrying to sit elsewhere. Settling herself next to the window, leaving Zolanda to sort out where to put their bags, Dolly said, 'Right driver, you can go now,' which he did, causing Zolanda to hang on tightly, as she had not yet sat down.

The tour apparently came with commentary on interesting sites, and they both seemed to enjoy hearing all the interesting things relayed to them by the driver. Before they knew it, the bus drew into a parking space at

Lake Windermere. Rising from his seat and addressing his temporary flock, the driver said, 'Ladies and Gentlemen, as you know, the tour includes a cruise on the lake, and if you look over my shoulder you will see the craft waiting for you. The cruise lasts for one and a half hours, and I'll be parked right here on your return. You just have to show the chap on the dock your ticket. Have a pleasant trip, and see you in a while.'

They all climbed down from the bus, hurrying over the grass and onto the dock where the appointed boat lay peacefully, rocking gently in the waves. As Dolly and Zolanda had been at the back of the bus, they were at the end of the queue for seats on board, much to Dolly's annoyance. By the time they had boarded, all the seats outside were taken, people ready with their cameras, wiping on sunscreen for it was one of those elusive and rare things, a beautiful English summer's day. With no choice, Dolly and Zolanda had to move inside which, because of the heat, was reminiscent of a sauna. 'Holy Hannah, I'm going to die in here,' said Dolly. 'Someone will have to move, I can't stand this.' When the driver came inside to do whatever drivers do to start the engine, she said, 'Get someone to move so I can sit outside, I can't stand this heat.'

'I can't do that madam. All you can do is ask someone yourself if they would mind moving.' He turned knobs and flicked switches, the engine started, and they were off. The driver now mentally marked Dolly as that dreaded Awkward Passenger.

Out on the water the boat really started to rock, and despite the commentary provided on interesting sites, and because of the stifling heat inside the cabin, Dolly felt herself starting to nod off. Even when the snores became particularly loud, no one came to shake her awake, all aboard preferring Dolly's snores to Dolly

45

awake. The afternoon progressed. Zolanda went out on deck where a very nice man offered to stand so she could sit and take photographs without losing her balance. She was enjoying herself so much, she squashed over so the man could sit beside her, and looking out over the sparkling blue water thought, *it really doesn't get much better than this.*

4

Dolly awoke slowly, the dream instantly fading from memory. Sitting upright, she wiped her chin where she had appeared to have been dribbling. Looking round, she couldn't see Zolanda and thought she must be in the toilet. Calling to the driver to enquire, she was told they didn't have such a facility. As comprehension came to Dolly, she realised that meant Zolanda was no longer on board. But if she wasn't on board, where was she? They were still in the middle of the lake, heading for the dock where they had boarded. Standing up with difficulty in the rocking craft, she made her way to the man in charge. 'Well if she's not in the toilet, where is she?'

'She got off.'

'Got off? What do you mean "got off"? How could she get off, we're in the middle of the lake.'

'Madam, if you had been awake, you would have realised that we make several stops along the shore so passengers can get on and off.'

'Oh,' said Dolly. 'So you're telling me that my friend got off?'

'Yes madam.' Sigh.

'But where did she go?'

'I have no idea. We waited some ten minutes for her and she didn't return. When she got off she said she was going to stretch her legs, but when she didn't come back Jack and I decided she must be walking back to the pier, and we have a schedule to keep to. We couldn't wait around indefinitely.'

'But how long is it to walk back?' enquired Dolly.

'I dunno, I've never done it. I would think about an hour, wouldn't you Jack?' This last question was addressed to his shipmate sitting at the front. 'Yeah, about that,' was the reply. Both the driver and Jack obviously hadn't given any thought to it at all.

'But we're on a tour, what if she misses the bus?'

'I can't help you there, I'm just in charge of the boat,' and with that he picked up the microphone again and gave another interesting fact about the lake.

Dolly returned to her seat. She felt completely flummoxed. It just wasn't like Zolanda to take off without telling her. All right she'd been asleep, but Zolanda would have woken her up and told her she planned to walk back surely? This really was most insensitive of Zolanda causing her all this worry, and she would definitely give her a piece of her mind when they met up again. The sky had darkened, rain clouds threatened, did Zolanda have her raincoat with her? What would she do if it rained? Dolly hunted around under the seat and saw both her and Zolanda's carry bags, Zolanda's rain jacket visible. *Well, she's going to get wet,* she thought. *A silly woman who had made a silly decision, but so very typical of Zolanda.*

As the minutes ticked away and they drew nearer to the dock, Dolly felt sure she would see her friend standing there waiting for her. The boat bumped gently against the pier, and once it was tied up, the driver and Jack helped all the passengers off. Dolly now had to carry both bags, no one being of a mind to offer help, so getting her up the short ladder was an adventure for all. As the other passengers made their way over to the waiting bus, Dolly looked at the path along the side of the lake, and although there were people walking to and fro, there was still no sign of Zolanda.

Back at the bus, she said, 'My friend has decided to walk back, but she isn't here yet so you'll have to wait.'

'I can't do that, I've got a timetable to keep to. I can't keep all these people waiting just because your friend can't get back in time,' said the driver, following the other eight passengers on board.

'You can't go yet, what will happen to Zolanda?'

'Are you getting on or aren't you? I'm late as it is so make your mind up. You can wait for her over in the café there,' he said, pointing to a wooden shed with a few tables outside.

Now Dolly was even more confused. A quick decision was required, never one of Dolly's strengths. Should she go on the bus and hope Zolanda found her own way back, which would serve her right, or should she stay and wait for her? Decisions, decisions.

'So what's it going to be?' asked the driver, the other passengers starting to look rebellious at being held up after a long day.

'I'll come with you, take these bags I can't manage both of them on my own,' and with the decision made, Dolly climbed aboard. As the bus reversed to exit the car park, Dolly again looked back in search of her friend, but again there was no sign.

Back at the hotel, Dolly lugged both bags, with difficulty, into the lobby. 'Has my friend come back?' she asked the receptionist.

'I haven't seen her,' was the reply. Tutting loudly, Dolly left one of the bags behind the desk for collection later, and laboured her way up the stairs. Three stops along the way, she reached the third floor. First she knocked on Zolanda's door, number 307, but there was no reply. Now Dolly was getting annoyed. 'I bet she's getting something to eat,' she said out loud, 'just wait till I get hold of her,' and opening her door, number 305, she dumped the bag and headed back downstairs. A search of the public rooms didn't reveal her friend, however.

What was she to do now? Should she call somebody? But what would she say? 'My friend, Zolanda, is missing from the boat. She said she was going for a walk at one of the stops but never returned.' Would they think she was mad? Indecision gripped Dolly, and deciding that a drink was needed, she entered the bar. For once the barman was there, and she ordered a gin and tonic with ice, and sat at a table to think. Unfortunately the drink and all the worry had made her sleepy, so climbing the stairs once more, hauling herself up by her good hand, she sank onto the bed and slept.

At six thirty, Dolly resurfaced. Feeling peckish, she wondered why Zolanda hadn't woken her for dinner. Then she remembered Zolanda hadn't returned on the boat. Thinking she had to have made her way to the hotel by now, by whatever means, Dolly left her room and knocked on Zolanda's door. There was no reply. It was at this point that a small worry worm entered Dolly's head. Obviously something had happened to Zolanda, and whatever it was, it concerned the lake. Should she go back there now or should she call the police? Would the police think she was a nutcase? Did she care if they did? Absolutely not, her friend was in trouble and Dolly had to help. Turning to the telephone beside the bed, Dolly asked the hotel operator for an outside line. Hearing the dial tone, and for the first time in her life, she dialled 999.

'Which service do you want?'

'Police.' After a couple of clicks she heard, 'Police, Sergeant Collins speaking, is this an emergency?'

'Yes,' replied Dolly and relayed the details. 'So she isn't back yet and I'm worried about her,' she said, at the end of explaining how Zolanda had disappeared.

'And when did this happen madam?'

'This afternoon.'

'We can't treat her as a missing person until twenty-four hours have passed. Please call back at that time.'

Dolly couldn't believe her ears. 'You've got to be kidding!' she said. 'I can't wait for twenty-four hours, I need someone to go and look for her now.'

'We can't do that madam. She may have decided to take a little break and would be most upset if the police started looking for her. What I will do is have the constable who looks after that area keep an eye out for her, unofficial like. Now give me a description,' and Dolly was left with no choice but to provide it.

'Well, she's about sixty-five, grey hair, rather long and untidy looking, she really needs to get it cut.'

'Yes madam, but we want a full physical description, colour of eyes, that sort of thing.'

'Oh, well it would have been helpful if you'd have said that at the beginning. She's not too fat, not too thin, sort of average really. About my height.'

'And what height would that be madam?' asked the sergeant, thinking this was like pulling trout's teeth. He thought in fish, being an avid fisherman.

'There's no need to be snippy constable, I'm doing my best.'

'It's Sergeant madam, Sergeant Collins. Height?'

'About five foot four,' adding that extra inch.

'Colour of eyes?'

'Blueish greyish, a hazel colour really, well browny I think. I can't say I've ever taken much notice actually.'

'I see madam. What was she wearing?'

'Now let me think. It wasn't very warm, so it would

have been, let me see, um, I can't remember,' said Dolly.

The sergeant, wondering what he had done to deserve this trouble, sighed loudly, which was heard by Dolly.

'I don't like your attitude constable, you should do something about that, being in public service and everything.'

Biting back a reply, the sergeant said sarcastically, 'If you could think what she was wearing that would be helpful, this being tourist season you see.'

'Send someone out to the lake to have a look around, she must be there somewhere. You can call me back here, my name is Dolly Evans, and I'm staying at The Eagle Hotel in Morton-Next-the-Sea, room 305,' and she gave him the phone number.

Hanging up, the sergeant handed the piece of paper with Zolanda's details, such as they were, to his colleague. 'Ring Barry and tell him to look out for this old lady around Windermere will you?' That done, he returned to the stack of paperwork on his desk.

Dolly went down to the dining room at seven-fifteen, and once again had to wait, but this time the table was ready quickly, probably due to the foot tapping and coughing she was unable to resist while standing at the door. The waitress did her best, in Dolly's opinion, to ignore her, and when her meal eventually came it was lukewarm, the gravy had lumps in it and the carrots were as if raw. She selected sticky toffee pudding for dessert, with cream; it arrived minus the cream as they had 'run out'. Shaking her head in utter disbelief, she signed the bill and waddled her way back upstairs. Checking Zolanda's room, there was still no reply, so deciding there was little else she could do, she prepared for bed. Having to cope alone was the icing on the cake as far as she was concerned, and she went to bed thinking this was the last time she would take Zolanda away with her, she really was most inconsiderate. Munching on a secret stash of cookies she had hidden in one of her cases, unknown to Zolanda as she had no intention of sharing, she brushed the crumbs off the sheet and turning over, slept.

5

As the boat had drawn up at the small dock halfway around the lake, Zolanda looked at the young couple waiting to board. Obviously very much in love, they were dressed for hiking, limbs golden and healthy, both wearing shorts and carrying backpacks that looked heavy. They had been sitting on the grass watching the boat arrive, but as it approached they stood and made their way to the end of the dock. Their arms were around each other and Zolanda smiled to herself. Oh to be young again! The other crew-member on the boat, she thought he had said his name was Jack, jumped from the boat to the dock, tying off the front rope, then hurrying to the rear. The driver announced they would be here for ten minutes in case anyone wanted to stretch their legs. On the spur of the moment, Zolanda decided she would enjoy the chance to explore alone. Going into the cabin she retrieved her camera from her carry bag, and with Dolly still snoring, went outside and climbed on to the dock. Three other passengers had also disembarked, but they were content to stay near the boat enjoying the sun and taking photos while Zolanda wanted to walk, so waving at them and with every intention of staying nearby, after all she only had ten minutes, she checked her watch and set off down the path.

Within moments she was totally alone, no view of the lake or boat. She walked along the narrow path bordered

by tall grass and weedy shrubs. A rabbit darted in front
of her; obviously not used to seeing anyone here and
unsure what to do, it sat up and looked at her. Zolanda
stood still, not wanting to frighten the tiny thing. Twitch-
ing its nose, it jumped into the grass at the side of the
path. Zolanda continued to stand still, soaking in the
sound of the wind in the taller trees and the birdsong.
While Dolly was certainly difficult to get along with, it
was for moments like these that she felt grateful, and
reminded herself to thank Dolly for bringing her along
when she returned to the boat. Checking her watch – she
still had five minutes before she had to turn round –
she looked ahead. Seeing a large oak tree at a bend in
the path, she decided to walk that far then turn back. As
she approached the tree she heard shouting. *Oh dear,
someone doesn't seem very happy*, she thought, and as she
started to turn round to head back, something flashed
among the bushes. Parting them with her hands, she
looked through. A large clearing presented itself, a small
caravan towards the back with a Land Rover beside it.

Two men sitting on collapsible chairs had a large bag
and were taking something out of it, and whatever it was
caught the sun. Stepping back, her foot landed on a twig
and it broke with a loud crack. As she turned to head
back down the path she bumped into something. A man
stood in front of her, blocking her path.

'Ron, get over here, we've got company,' he called.
'Ron' appeared promptly, followed by the man who had
been taking things out of the bag. 'What have we here?'
he said. 'Doing a bit of snooping are you?'

'What? No, I was on the boat and wanted to stretch my
legs, that's all. I'll just be going back to the boat if you'll
let me pass,' she said to the man blocking her way, and
waited for him to move. He didn't.

'What do we do now Ron? She was peering through

the grass, she must have seen you. We can't let her go back to this here boat can we?'

'No Kenny we can't. Bring her over,' and with that Zolanda felt a large strong hand on her arm, another covering her mouth. Trying to say 'let me go', she found herself pushed through the bushes and into the clearing. The man holding her jerked her to a halt. 'What do we do with her?'

'She'll have to come with us, we can't let her go now.' She tried to get away from them, but now, held by two strong hands, it just wasn't possible. With no choice, she was led through the bushes.

Surely someone from the boat would come after her? They wouldn't just leave, they couldn't, Dolly wouldn't let them. Then she realised that Dolly was probably still sleeping and wouldn't even realise she was missing. She felt tears come to her eyes, her nose started to run, but with her arms held she was unable to wipe it. Zolanda felt very scared. 'Right, put her in the caravan for now while we decide what to do, and tie her hands and feet.' She was roughly pushed up through the door, the rough hands pulling her down to sit on a bench. Pulling a length of thin yellow rope out of a cupboard, the man called Kenny bound first her hands, then her feet. Looking around for some other way out, she realised with horror there wasn't one. The windows were tiny, certainly too small for her to climb through, and with no other door she could only sit on a chair and wait.

Outside, the three men stood around. 'Well, now we're in a mess. She must have seen what we were doing.' They looked at each other, each waiting for the other to come up with a good plan, but never having been in this situation before they didn't know how to deal with it. Ron, who appeared to be the one who made the decisions, said, 'We've got to get this stuff to the fence before it's reported stolen. Kenny, you stay here with her, she can't get out of the caravan, and it's getting late now, no one will come by. Sit outside the door and just stay here until we get back.'

'Oh no you don't,' said Kenny firmly. 'What's to stop you two taking off with the money and leaving me here babysitting? No way, we all go together.'

'Then what do we do with her?' asked Ron, pointing in the direction of the caravan. They continued to sit in deep thought, but as none of them were bright thinkers – if they were they wouldn't be in this mess – it was obviously going to take some time.

Zolanda sat alone. *Oh Dolly, where are you? They have to let me go, they can't keep me here all night,* and with that reassuring thought, she bucked herself up. Besides, Dolly would surely be looking for her.

The clock above the kitchen sink moved towards six o'clock, and Zolanda was hungry. With hands tied, her wrists were hurting with the rope tied too tightly; this was indeed a low moment for her. The door opened, and thinking they were coming to release her she tried to talk.

'Shut up lady, you're not going anywhere, I've just come to get something to eat,' and walking past her, Ron pulled a couple of bags of crisps out of the cupboard above the small sink, rummaged in the small fridge for three cans of beer, and walked out again. Zolanda, who was extremely hungry and was in need of a bathroom, felt the tears start to roll down her cheeks.

When Kenny appeared shortly after, he said, 'What's the matter?' Trying to say 'I need a bathroom', she could only make gurgling noises. Not understanding these, he walked into the tiny bathroom to use the facilities, and on coming out said, 'Do you need the bathroom?' She nodded her head violently. 'All right, but don't try anything funny. I'll untie your hands and feet, but I'll be right outside the door. Understand?' Nodding again, Zolanda waited while he untied the ropes and as soon as she was free made a dash for the bathroom. The window was tiny, little more than the size of a large dinner plate and she realised she had no hope of climbing out.

When she was finished, she opened the door. Kenny, true to his word, was standing outside, leaning against the fridge. 'Hold your hands out,' he said, and proceeded to retie her wrists. He made her sit on the chair again and retied her feet, but neither of the ropes felt as tight as before. She said, 'Can I have something to eat please? I'm very hungry.' Looking at her, Kenny said, 'I'll ask Ron,' and opening the door a crack said, 'This old lady wants something to eat Ron, she says she's hungry.'

'Well give her something then you idiot,' was the reply, and opening a cupboard, Kenny found a can of peanuts. Removing the lid, he put them on the bench next to Zolanda. 'Knock yourself out with those,' he said, and went outside to join the others.

Now they were in a dilemma. They had to get the stolen stuff to the fence, which would take a couple of hours at least. One wouldn't be trusted to go on his own in case he didn't return. They couldn't all go as they couldn't lock Zolanda in the caravan. Or could they? The windows, as already discussed, were too small to climb through, so that left the one door. Could it be locked from inside? Kenny went inside to check, and came out again immediately. Of course it could lock from inside, otherwise how could you sleep without worrying, but he couldn't work out if that would help them or not. The only way was to tie Zolanda up securely and all go into town together. Ron entered the caravan to find Zolanda on the floor trying to pick up the peanuts she had spilt, but with tied hands it was proving difficult. 'We have to leave for a while, so we're going to tie you to the table, just in case.'

'Please don't! Say there's a fire, I won't be able to get out.'

'No choice,' he said, and taking another length of rope from the same cupboard as before, he helped her up and pushed her onto the bench. Attaching the rope to the existing one at her wrists, he then tied the rope to the table leg, knotting it securely. A dirty handkerchief appeared from his trouser pocket and was tied around her mouth, Zolanda was trying so hard not to cry, but she was very scared. She was genuinely frightened of fire and was terrified something would happen while they were gone. Trying to ask them not to leave her, all that came out was a muffled noise, and Ron took no notice. At least the rope was long enough that she could stay on the bench, but other than that, she was totally immobile. Without another word he walked out, and she heard the door being locked after him. Looking around, she couldn't even see out of a window, all she could do was wait and pray that Dolly would come looking for her.

6

Dolly woke early, her first thought of Zolanda. What had the silly woman done? Surely she must be wandering out by the lake somewhere? She thought back to her conversation with the policeman – what was his name? Constable Higgins? No, that wasn't it. Sergeant? Sergeant Higgins? Dolly couldn't remember, but no doubt they would have a file on Zolanda by now. Looking at the bedside clock she saw it was only seven-thirty, but the police were always on duty so she saw no reason to wait until later. Picking up the phone she waited for the hotel operator. And waited. And waited. Where was this person? Why wasn't someone answering?

Deciding to go to reception, she put on her dressing gown, luckily she had bought a clean one with her, and put her feet into her slippers. Taking the room key, she went downstairs. 'Hello?' she called, but there was no reply. 'HELLO?'

From behind the desk a door opened, and Trevor poked his head out. Collar undone and tie loosened, he was rubbing his eyes. 'Yes, what do you want?'

'Young man, I've been trying to get an outside line, but now it's clear why I couldn't, you were sleeping on duty weren't you?'

'I was not, I'm just rubbing my eyes.'

'I don't have time to get into a discussion with you on the perils of telling fibs, we'll save that for later. Now get me an outside line, I need to call the police.'

Instantly Trevor was awake. 'Police? Why, what's wrong? Are you ill?'

'If I was ill I would probably be dead by now I've been waiting so long, now give me the line,' and picking up the telephone on the desk she glared at Trevor. Hearing the dial tone, she again asked for the police, and as soon as she was connected said, 'Have you found Zolanda yet?'

'Beg pardon madam?' said Constable Roberts.

'I *said*, have you found Zolanda yet?'

'Madam, may I have your name?'

'Dolly Evans. I was talking to a constable or a sergeant, I can't remember which, last night. He said he would have someone have a look around the lake.'

'Just a moment madam, let me check the files.' Putting the call on hold, he said, 'Here Tom, there's some woman on the phone by the name of Dolly Evans. Wants to know if we've found someone called Zolanda yet?'

'She's up early,' said Tom Collins. 'She called last night about her friend, got lost around Windermere apparently. I asked Barry to go and have a quick look, but he couldn't find her. I told her to call back when twenty-four hours were up.'

Back on the telephone with Dolly, Constable Roberts said, 'No madam, we have found no trace of your friend yet. I understand she hasn't been missing for twenty-four hours yet, and we can't really do anything until then.'

'Oh for goodness sake, what good is it having a police force if they won't do anything!' and she put the phone down.

Dolly made a decision: it was going to be up to her to find Zolanda.

Dressed and ready to leave by seven-thirty, Dolly decided that if she was to find Zolanda she would need a good breakfast first, and standing at the dining room door she saw the room was empty. She could hear clattering and talking coming from the kitchen, so knew someone was around, but after a few moments no one had appeared. She was very reluctant to go too near the swinging kitchen doors, so standing just out of range she called, 'Hello?' Eventually the young waitress looked through the round window in the door, and came out to speak to her.

'Yes?'

'I want my breakfast.'

'We haven't started serving yet.'

'Well start now. I want a pot of coffee and three slices of toast.' Dolly sat down at a table, staring at the young girl who went back into the kitchen. A moment later the chef's face appeared at the window, obviously wanting to see the person that was so demanding. Dolly just stared back at him, waiting for her food. She wasn't sure how she was going to go about this, never having lost a friend around a lake before. The first hurdle would be to get to the lake, so while waiting for her breakfast she went back out to the reception desk. 'Trevor?' she called. Trevor appeared through the door, his shirt and tie properly presented. 'Order a taxi for me to be here in an hour. I'm going to Windermere.' She returned to the dining room and her fortifying meal, Trevor standing looking after her, pitying the inhabitants of Windermere.

Breakfast over, she waited in the lobby for the taxi. As luck would have it, it was the same driver who had brought her and Zolanda to the hotel, and he groaned loudly when he saw her emerge from the hotel. 'Lake Windermere, driver, the pier where the cruise boats leave from.' She climbed into the back seat.

Stan Gibbons had been driving his taxi in the Lake District for some thirty years, and knew every road, lane, and shortcut in that beautiful part of the world. Things went well until Dolly thought she knew a quicker way and demanded he take it. 'That doesn't go to Windermere,' he said when she pointed to a small lane.

'It must do, I'm sure the lake is over in that direction.'

'Well it's not, I know where I'm going.'

'That I very much doubt. I'm in a hurry, why are you dawdling along? Doesn't this thing go any faster?'

'Not when there's a police car behind it doesn't,' said Stan, and turning round in her seat, Dolly indeed saw a white car, 'Police' written in large letters on a roof sign.

'Stop the car, I want to speak to them.'

'I can't just stop here, I'll be blocking traffic.'

'I said stop the car!' So Stan did. Fortunately the police driver, just having completed a refresher course, had been well trained in avoiding accidents and he managed to swerve just in time to miss the taxi's back bumper by mere inches. Dolly's door and the police driver's door both opened simultaneously.

'What the hell do you think you're doing?' said the policeman. 'You can't stop here, you're blocking traffic.'

By now the taxi driver had also appeared. 'I told her that, but she wouldn't listen officer, just insisted I stop, said she wanted to speak to you,' and he leaned his bottom against the side door, looking forward to the coming battle.

'Have you found Zolanda yet constable?'

'Madam, you can't have this car stopped in the middle of the road. I insist you move on until you come to a lay-by,' replied Constable Gibson.

'But ...'

'No, MOVE THE CAR.'

So climbing back into the taxi, both driver and passenger progressed along the winding road, keeping exactly to the speed limit much to Dolly's annoyance, until a lay-by presented itself. Drawing in, the driver watched the police car follow them to a stop. Dolly was out of the car as quickly as she was able, and stood waiting. She could see the officer was on the phone, but that didn't stop her banging on the window to get his attention. He continued speaking to the powers that be, asking if anyone knew anything about a Zolanda. Upon hearing of a formidable harridan who had reported the unfortunate misplacing of a friend of the aforementioned name at Windermere the day before, he was quickly brought up to speed, and now felt in possession of enough facts to face Dolly.

Out of the car, he towered over Dolly. 'Madam, what was it you wanted?'

'I asked if your lot had found my friend Zolanda yet. We were on a boat ride on Windermere yesterday and she left the boat for a stroll at one of the piers while I was having a short nap. She never returned. I called the police but they said I had to wait for twenty-four hours before reporting it, which is utterly ridiculous. So, have you found her yet?'

'No madam, apparently not.'

'Right, well, since the police aren't doing their job I'll have to do it for you,' and she headed back to the taxi.

'Madam, I would advise you to follow the rules. If your friend has now been missing for the stipulated twenty-four hours, you are better to go to the station and file a Missing Person Report.'

'And what good is that going to do, young man?'

'That means we can then begin a search, but we're going to need all the details of your friend, Until we have those, we don't know who we're looking for.' Thinking with a clearer head this morning, Dolly could see the sense in this for once. Should she continue on her own to the lake, or should she do as advised and file a report? The twenty-four hours weren't up yet, but would be shortly, and deciding to get the facts on paper prior to that, she said, 'All right, I'll come with you, drive to the station.'

'I'm on patrol Madam, I can't do that.'

'Don't be ridiculous, young man. You just told me to go to the police station and file a report, now you're telling me you can't take me there.' Walking around the car, and before he could stop her, Dolly opened the door and with some difficulty sat in the passenger seat. The policeman and the taxi driver looked at each other, both shaking their heads. It wasn't until Stan, the taxi driver, was halfway back to Morton that he realised Dolly hadn't paid for the ride. Thinking about it he was grateful for his lucky escape and decided to look on the trip as a nice drive in the country. He began whistling a happy tune.

In the police car Constable Gibson was on the phone telling dispatch that he was heading to the local police station with a person who would want to file a Missing Person Report. It seemed that most people had now heard of Dolly, and it was lucky for everyone that she didn't hear the laughter on the other end of the phone.

The police station proved to be some thirty minutes drive away and Dolly felt it a good use of the time to tell her driver of the events leading up to Zolanda's disappearance. It was thus with relief that Constable Gibson drove into the parking lot, and showing Dolly to the main desk beat a hasty retreat in pursuit of a bracing cup of tea.

'I want to file a Missing Person Report,' she said to the duty sergeant.

'Yes madam, how long has this person been missing?'

'Twenty-two hours.'

'I see.' Drawing out from beneath his desk the right forms and licking his stubby pencil, he asked, 'Name?'

'Dolly Evans.'

'Height?'

'Five foot four. Why do you need to know how tall I am?'

'I don't madam. I thought you said you had a Missing Person?'

'I do.'

'Then I want to know their details.'

'Do you mean Zolanda's?'

'Yes madam.' Dolly thought this was said in a somewhat rude way, but guessed, rightly, that the man must have a very difficult job having to deal with difficult people and so decided to let it go.

'Let's start again,' said the sergeant, tearing up that form and drawing a new one from the pile. 'Name?'

'Zolanda Nerling.' Dolly continued to give details – five foot five, blueish brownish hazel eyes, grey hair, sixty-five years old, unkindly stating that she hadn't weathered well. As to clothes, she thought she had been wearing a print skirt but as to colour, she had no idea. If it was any help to the police she didn't have her rain jacket with her, at which point the sergeant could no longer contain himself and just looked at her, shaking his head.

'Right madam, can you remember where your friend got off the boat?'

'Of course I can't. I already told the constable that I was sleeping, but the man who drove the boat would remember I'm sure.'

'Which boat was it madam?'

'Huh?'

'Boat madam, there are many on the lake, which one were you on?'

'How do you expect me to remember that! It was a boat at the pier. Somebody named Jack was driving it I think.'

Sighing loudly, the sergeant called into the room behind him, 'Frank, come here a minute will you?', and on Frank's appearance said, 'We have a Missing Person Report. Disappeared yesterday from the main pier on Windermere. Get on the phone and ask Jack on his boat about this 'ere lady that's gone missing.'

'Right Sergeant.'

Dolly remained at the desk, irritatingly drumming her fingers to a tune known only to herself, annoying the sergeant into exquisite agony until eventually Frank returned. 'He's on a trip. The office said it would be best to go and speak to him directly,' and with that task accomplished, Frank returned to the back room.

'Right, in that case I'm coming too,' said Dolly.

'No madam, leave it to us. Where are you staying?'

'The Eagle Hotel in Grange. I'm not going anywhere until you find Zolanda.' True to her word she looked around for a comfortable seat and squeezed into it, her purse on her ample lap, the pink plaster cast resting on top of her purse.

Sometimes the wheels of bureaucracy grind exceedingly slowly, but today they ramped themselves up splendidly, and Dolly watched and listened as orders were given and a car and policewoman departed for the lake. Dolly sat and watched various people come in, one to report a missing cat (tabby, answers to the name of Pumpkin), another a stolen bicycle. She watched the hands on the clock go steadily round until she would have killed for a cup of tea and something to eat, but she was reluctant to leave her post should news suddenly arrive.

Another half hour came and went, until Dolly said, 'Sergeant, where can I get a cup of tea and something to eat?'

'Turn right outside the door, there's a small café that

does a nice line in sausage sandwiches,' and he returned to his numerous, unseen tasks.

Dolly found the café as described. Sitting at a table for two, she was quickly attended to, deciding on the Super Sausage Sandwich, which came with beans and chips, and a pot of tea. Her meal came surprisingly quickly and indeed lived up to the police sergeant's recommendation. She also asked for a sticky bun in a paper bag to be added to her bill, one never knew when hunger pangs would strike and it was best to be prepared.

Dolly paid her bill and headed back to the station. Still no news. The afternoon stretched on, and Dolly's back and other regions were aching with the hard seat. Privately she wondered what she would do if there was no news by tonight, but didn't want to voice her thoughts, the alternative was too horrible to contemplate. She indeed looked the epitome of an unhappy elderly lady to all who saw her.

7

Kenny, Ron, and the third member of this outlaw band – who was named Christopher by his parents some twenty-two years prior but was now known by the sobriquet 'Pinky' – had left the caravan site half an hour earlier. Ron, the self-appointed leader, had gathered up the various articles to be taken to the fence and loaded everything onto the back seat of the van, covered over with an old tartan picnic blanket.

'I'm not happy leaving that old woman on her own Ron,' said Kenny. 'She's right, what would happen if there was a fire, she might die.'

'Give over Ken, there's nothing to start a fire. She'll be fine till we get back and we won't be long. If Malcolm is in we can be there and back inside a couple of hours. We must get this stuff to him before it's listed as stolen,' and he continued to speed along as fast as his old van would go, down the road to Kendal.

Kenny lifted the corner of the blanket and looked at the haul. It included a matching pair of old silver candlesticks that should get a good price, a silver cigarette box, a Georgian coffee pot that was outstanding in its beauty. Kenny, the more cerebral of the trio, if such could be said, hoped none of these pieces would be melted down. He knew it happened, but in his heart of hearts he wasn't a bad man, just an ill-advised and weak one. Ron and Pinky now, they were of a different breed, and Kenny worried about the old lady back in the caravan. What was going to happen to her? Ron was a nasty piece of work when people upset him or when he was cornered, he'd been known to beat up people just for looking at him the wrong way. Kenny had come up against this side of him on a couple of occasions and didn't wish to go down that road again, but he was worried about the old lady. What could he do to help, preferably without letting Ron know it was him? Putting his not-considerable brain to work, he spent the rest of the journey trying to find a way.

8

It was very quiet when the three men left. Zolanda had only really seen Ron and Kenny. The third one, Pinky, seemed to be on the periphery of all the events. It was obvious Ron was the ringleader, but it seemed to her upon reflection that Kenny wasn't happy with having to tie her up, especially when she said she was frightened of fire. When evening came and they still weren't back, it was pitch black outside the window, even blacker inside. She desperately needed to go to the bathroom again, but tied as she was it was impossible, so she tried to keep as still as possible, but that just led to cramp in her leg. For the first time, Zolanda wept.

It was with relief that she heard the van drive back at about eight o'clock, and the first one through the door was Ron, followed by Kenny and Pinky. Zolanda's mouth ached with the handkerchief binding it, and looking at all three she tried to tell them she needed the bathroom.

'What's she saying?' asked Pinky.

'I think she probably needs the bathroom,' said Kenny. 'Is that right?' and she nodded vigorously. Untying arms and legs couldn't happen quickly enough for her, and she fairly flew into the bathroom, tears still coursing down her face. She removed the gag, she didn't care if they did put it back at this point, she just wanted to relieve the pain in her mouth. Again she stared at the window, but it hadn't grown in size, so despondently she went back outside. 'Please don't use that gag again, it really hurts,' she said.

'If you promise not to shout,' said Ron.

'Yes, I promise,' she replied, feeling as if she was giving a Girl Guide promise not to litter. If only that were true.

It appeared that while they had been gone they had decided on sleeping arrangements for the night. Zolanda would continue to be tied to the table and Ron would sleep in the only bedroom at the end of the caravan. It contained a large double bed, ample room for two, but Kenny and Pinky had been relegated to sleeping in the van, a decision that obviously didn't sit well with either of them. With Ron snoring in the bedroom, Zolanda found herself nodding off, uncomfortable though she was, waking fitfully through the night as she tried to move to ease a cramp but unable to because of the ropes.

The next morning came none too soon for Zolanda and the two in the van. Ron slept blissfully on, however, even when Kenny and Pinky came into the caravan to look for food. Zolanda decided to try again to plead for her release while Ron was out of the way. 'Please let me go, I promise I won't tell anyone about you.'

'We can't do that,' said Pinky. 'Ron would be mad, he's the one that makes the decisions around here.'

'But can't you see how bad this will be for you? He's making all the wrong decisions, and taking you along with him. Just untie the ropes and let me slip out, he won't know you helped me, really he won't.'

Kenny and Pinky looked at each other, both uncertain.

'You know this is kidnapping don't you? If you let me go, and if you were to be caught sometime, I could say that it was Ron who made you do all this.' She could see them both wavering, looking between her and the closed bedroom door where Ron still slept. 'Come on, quickly, before he wakes up.'

Kenny, to whom the whole thing had been wrong, said, 'Come on Pinky, she's right. You do her hands, I'll do her feet,' and they both set to. Zolanda could hardly contain herself, willing them to hurry before Ron appeared. They both seemed to have cauliflower thumbs and she could have screamed she was so tense. Pinky looked at her, the rope almost undone. 'What will we say to him?'

'Say you were sleeping, I must have got away during the night. Go back into the van and stay there until he appears. Quickly, there's no time left. Oh hurry do!'

The last rope undone, Zolanda made a dash for the caravan door, and was down the steps and along the path before either of them could say any more. She knew the path was only about five minutes from the lake, and all the time was praying that someone would be around. She could feel her heart thumping in her chest. *Hurry, hurry,* she told herself. *Don't look back, just hurry.*

As she broke through the bushes by the small pier she saw a boat. She didn't notice the name of it, all she saw was a policewoman, and shouting and waving her arms, she tried to run, run to safety.

9

With Kenny on the van's middle bench, and Pinky on the rear one, they both lay down, alert for the sound of the caravan door opening. 'What do you think he'll say?' said Pinky.

'Well he's not going to be pleased, I can tell you that much.'

'He's going to ask how she escaped.'

'We have our story ready. The old lady must have loosened the ropes during the night and slipped out. We didn't hear her, we were both sleeping. We know nothing. Besides, she promised she wouldn't say anything didn't she?'

'And you believe her? How long do you think she's been gone?'

'Yes, I do. About a couple of hours I think, but I didn't look at my watch when she legged it.' They both lapsed back into silence, ears aching with the effort of listening for Ron. Full daylight was now upon them, and they both began to wonder how much longer Ron could sleep. They were fed up with lying in the van, it wasn't exactly comfortable, and both of them were hungry. 'I'm starving,' said Pinky.

'Me too. He can't be much longer, the damn birds are making enough racket to wake the dead.' No sooner said than done, the caravan door opened and Ron exploded out. 'Where the hell's the old lady?' he shouted.

Kenny, wiping his eyes as though just waking up, sat up and stretched. 'What do you mean where's the old lady? She's in the caravan.'

'No she ain't, she's gone. Didn't you hear her leaving?'

'You were the one sleeping right next to her Ron, you sent us out to the van if you remember, where we spent a very uncomfortable, not to say chilly night.'

'Bloody hell, now we're in a mess! We have to get out of here fast. She'll be bringing the coppers round any minute now,' and he raced back inside.

Kenny and Pinky looked at each other, both of them giving a huge sigh. 'It looks as if we got away with it Kenny,' said Pinky.

'Don't count your chickens yet, not till we're out of here.' They both clambered out of the van. Ron was in the bedroom dressing, and looking out into the kitchen said, 'What do you think you're doing?'

'Getting something to eat, we're hungry.'

'We haven't got time to eat, you morons, we've got to get out of here.' Pushing them both aside he went out to back the van up to the caravan hitch. Kenny and Pinky continued to forage through the cupboards, and felt the caravan move as the hitch snagged on. Both grabbing some sliced bread, they went outside. And came face to face with two very large and ominous-looking policemen.

'Hello, hello, hello, what have we here?' said the larger one. 'If it isn't Kenny O'Hara himself, and Pinky Smith, good morning gentlemen.'

When they both looked to the right, two more policemen were standing either side of the van, smiling threateningly to the despondent figure inside, his hands on the wheel and looking very glum. 'Come along lads, we're going for a little ride.'

They were all cautioned, then, their hands in cuffs, all

three were walked along the path to the lake, there to find a police boat and the still-present cruise boat, Zolanda sitting beside the policewoman in the gently rocking craft.

10

Dolly could hear lots of people talking. Well, to be truthful, there was quite a bit of shouting, but she couldn't make out the words. She had already eaten the sticky bun she had purchased from the café, and was just thinking that another would go down quite nicely, when she heard her name called. 'Miss Evans, could you come through please?' Looking up she saw the sergeant holding open a door, and gathering up her purse she followed him through. 'Just take a seat here a moment please madam, the Inspector won't keep you long,' and he departed through yet another door leading to parts unknown.

Well at least they have an Inspector involved, better late than never, thought Dolly. *Oh dear, I hope it's not bad news, I don't think I can stand it if it is. I don't know what I'd do without Zolanda, even though she is terribly annoying at times, especially with that awful negative attitude of hers. But I would miss her terribly.* Sinking even deeper into this pit of gloom, she stared at the floor, feeling tears come to her eyes, and taking out her hankie she gave a gargantuan blow of her nose.

'Oh Dolly, it is good to hear you!' Looking up, she saw Zolanda.

'Zolanda, I thought you were dead,' she said, hardly daring to believe her eyes. 'Is it really you?'

'Yes Dolly, it's really me. What an adventure! I can't wait to tell you all about it, and the policemen tell me that it's partly thanks to you that I'm safe. They said you just wouldn't take no for an answer. I told them that my friend Dolly would rescue me, and so you did! Thank you Dolly.' And without more ado Zolanda put her arms around as much of Dolly as she could, and the two friends cried with relief.

Zolanda had to leave Dolly again to fill out a report, all of which to Dolly seemed to take much longer than necessary, but eventually they were told they were free to go back to their hotel, a police car and driver were standing by. Walking from the station with her good arm linked through Zolanda's, Dolly found she couldn't speak, she was totally overcome with joy at having her friend back with her again. Zolanda on the other hand was speaking enough for both of them, chattering away nineteen to the dozen about everything that had happened, who'd said what, and when, how she hadn't been scared, well, not much. Dolly let it all flow over her, just grateful that she could see and touch Zolanda again, and during the journey back to their hotel silently vowed never to be short with anyone ever again.

Back at The Eagle Hotel, Trevor was on duty as they entered the reception area. 'Trevor, have someone come to the bar, we wish to order a drink,' said Dolly.

'The bar's closed, the roof's leaking.'

'Perhaps you didn't hear me young man. I *said*, have someone come to the bar, we wish to order a drink.'

'I heard you, but you'll have to have it in the residents' lounge. As I *said*, the roof's leaking in the bar.' Trevor's attention immediately returned to the computer screen, a reflection of Solitaire showing in his glasses.

Dolly, still pleased at having found Zolanda again, decided not to make an issue of it, and they headed to the lounge. When approached by the waiter from the bar as to their requirements, Dolly ordered a bottle of champagne. 'Champagne, Dolly?' said Zolanda.

'Yes, this is a celebration,' and the two friends toasted each other, drinking until Dolly felt her eyes would pop.

Word soon got around the hotel about Dolly and Zolanda being returned in a police car, and as everyone knows, everyone knows everyone in Cumbria, so it wasn't long before the whole story was known to the staff. With each telling the story changed, an international gang of bank robbers involved in one, Russian spies involved in another, but the truth, known to Dolly and Zolanda, was more than enough for them, thank you. A table was reserved for them for dinner, the waiters attentive, the chef once again peeking through the dreaded kitchen doors to see the two ladies who had thwarted an international incident. Dolly and Zolanda sailed upstairs to bed without stopping once, borne on a cloud of good feelings all round. Both slept long and well, Dolly, remembering her silent vow not to be sharp with Zolanda again, bit her tongue when, helping her get dressed for breakfast, Zolanda caught Dolly's hair in the zipper of her dress, though it took all her resolve.

With one more day of their holiday left, they both decided they had had enough adventures and spent it quietly. A walk to the sea – they gave the bandstand a wide berth – coffee in a quaint little shop near the doctor's surgery, a snooze in the afternoon, and before they knew it, it was their last dinner at The Eagle Hotel.

'Well Zolanda, I must say it's been an experience coming away with you,' said Dolly.

'I know! Who would have thought we could have had such a good time, Dolly? It has been fun hasn't it? I must admit I was a bit nervous about coming away with you, you just never know if you're going to get on with someone do you? I mean, it's different from spending a day or something with them, but I must admit, this has been a wonderful holiday. Thank you ever so much for bringing me. I'm sorry you broke your wrist, but it all turned out for the best.'

Dolly wasn't sure about that, and would be even more unsure when she received the bill from the hotel, but all in all Zolanda was right, it had been a wonderful holiday.

Zolanda would need to come back to testify at the trial for the three kidnappers, and on reflection she found she was even sorrier for Kenny and Pinky. She had promised them she would speak on their behalf and she intended to keep to her promise. Besides which, it would mean another trip to the Lake District, and that couldn't be bad could it?

The morning of their departure came and, as predicted, Dolly wasn't happy with the bill, but try as she might, and she did try, she could find nothing wrong with it and reluctantly laid down her charge card. In the taxi back to Morton-Next-the-Sea station she said to Zolanda, 'Do you think I could come back when you have to testify?'

'Of course Dolly! What fun is a holiday by yourself?'

And they smiled at each other.

Diane Keziah Robertson